Lovers in Lisbon

G·K
Hall
&Co.

Also by Barbara Cartland
in Large Print:

Alone in Paris
Beyond the Stars
A Dream from the Night
The Eyes of Love
Forced to Marry
The Incomparable
Love and War
The Loveless Marriage
No Time For Love
Passage to Love
The Queen of Hearts
Saved by a Saint
Too Precious to Lose
The Wings of Ecstasy

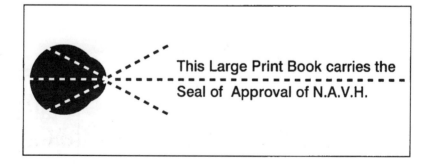

This Large Print Book carries the
Seal of Approval of N.A.V.H.

LOVERS IN LISBON

Barbara Cartland

G.K. Hall & Co. • Thorndike, Maine

Published in 2000 by arrangement with
International Book Marketing, Ltd.

G.K. Hall Large Print Paperback Series.

The text of this Large Print edition is unabridged.
Other aspects of the book may vary from the original edition.

Set in 16 pt. Plantin by Rick Gundberg.

Printed in the United States on permanent paper.

Library of Congress Cataloging-in-Publication Data

Cartland, Barbara, 1902–
   Lovers in Lisbon / Barbara Cartland.
     p.   cm.
   ISBN 0-7838-8929-1 (lg. print : sc : alk. paper)
   1. Lisbon (Portugal) — Fiction. 2. Large type books. I. Title.
 PR6005.A765 L657 2000
   823′.912—dc21
                                                   99-054983

Author's Note

If legends are to be believed, Lisbon was founded by Ulysses, but it is true that the Greeks traded along the Iberian coast and the great harbour of the River Tagus was for a long time called Olissibona — a name which is to be found on some of the earliest printed maps.

Lisbon to-day, with its semi-circle of seven hills sheltering the narrow flat land on the slow-flowing tidal river is extremely beautiful.

The people are smiling and welcoming, the fish, fresh and delicious in the Restaurants and the Churches have an atmosphere which speaks of the faith of its people which has remained unchanged over the centuries.

The narrow pavements in the Old City are crowded by a colourful throng of tourists; the hawkers of lottery tickets, the blind street singer with his guitar, the fruit pedlar with his barrow.

Flowers are sold around the splashing fountains of Rossio and the smell of coffee wafts from the Cafes to mingle with the sharp, sultry breeze from the sea.

It is all very unlike the hustle and bustle of more modern Cities and far more attractive.

Outside Lisbon, Estoril with its Villas, expensive hotels, flowered terraces and elegant shops has become the home of many European Monarchs and Royalty who have lost their thrones.

But while the last King of Portugal has gone, and with him most of the Court, a small creek still bears the name "Queen's Beach".

Chapter One
1890

The Manager stepped forward eagerly.

Down the stairs, moving with a grace that had been acclaimed all over Europe, came the *Duchesse de* Monreuil.

"Good-morning, *Madame,*" he said in French.

She replied in Portuguese, which was his own language:

"Good-morning, *Senhor,* it is a beautiful day!"

"Beautiful, *Madame,*" he replied, "for the sun shines wherever you go."

She smiled at him, and he said:

"The special carriage I have ordered will be arriving in a few minutes, and perhaps, *Madame,* you would prefer to wait in the Salon?"

"No, I will wait here," the *Duchesse* replied.

She seated herself as she spoke in an arm-chair in front of a writing-desk.

It stood in the centre of the large Reception Hall of the Grand Hotel.

She looked very attractive as she did so, wearing a gown which had obviously come from Paris.

Precious stones glittered in her small ears and on the long, thin fingers of her ungloved hand.

"Tell me," she said as the Manager hovered near her, "what has been happening in Lisbon since I was last here?"

Even as she asked the question she thought it was a mistake.

How could she bear to talk of Lisbon.

The last time she had stayed in what had been called the most beautiful City in Europe she had suffered an agony of misery she wanted to forget.

It had not been beautiful to her then.

Yet it seemed ridiculous that it was thirty-two years since she had last set foot in the country of her birth.

She remembered, she thought, every brick and stone of Lisbon.

The sunshine on the sea, the beauty of the ancient buildings, the flowers which were everywhere.

Especially she recalled those in the sellers' baskets around the stone fountains.

When she had arrived last night and smelt the familiar fragrance that was especially Lisbon she knew she had made a mistake.

Her first impulse therefore on waking this morning was to leave immediately and return to Paris.

Yet, having forced herself to come to the country, now that she was here her pride, which was very much part of her character, would not let her play the coward.

Once and for all she would lay 'the ghost' that had haunted her for so long.

A ghost which she was afraid she would carry to her grave.

She had tried to forget when she was being acclaimed in France, in Monte Carlo, in Greece, in Hungary, in Vienna and in London.

She had told herself that she would not think of him, she would not remember.

And yet he was always there.

If she closed her eyes she could see his handsome face as if it was yesterday.

"Darling little Inès, I love you!" It was his deep voice echoing down the years. "You are mine, mine completely, and I am the first and the only man in your life."

Prophetic words.

So prophetic that she felt even now when she was approaching old age like screaming because she could not escape from him.

With an effort she brought her thoughts back from the past.

The Manager was still standing near her chair.

"Tell me," she said, "now that the *Marques* Juan de Oliveira Vasconles is dead, who is living in the Palace da Azul?"

"His son, *Madame,* the *Marques* Alvaro now lives there."

"His son!" The *Duchesse* repeated the words beneath her breath. "I did not know he had a son."

"*Si Si, Madame,* the *Marques* Alvaro is very like his father. Very handsome, very charming and — let me see — he must be over thirty by now."

9

"I had no idea," the *Duchesse* said in a faint voice.

"*Madame* must have met the *Marques* Juan when you were last here?"

For a moment the *Duchesse* closed her eyes.

Then she said in a voice that did not sound like her own:

"Yes . . . I met him."

"You will recollect, *Madame*, how magnificent the *Marques* looked when riding his superb horses."

"And the new *Marques* . . . his son?"

"He looks like his father, and as a rider is admired by every young man in the whole country, while his horses win all our most important races."

The Manager smiled before he added: ·

"We are very proud of the *Marques* Alvaro, just as we were proud of his father."

Again the *Duchesse* closed her eyes.

She could see the *Marques* as the Manager had described him, riding towards her on a huge black horse.

The moment she had seen him it was as if he had stepped down from the mountains.

The simple people still believed they were the habitation of the gods.

He was certainly god-like to her.

God-like from the moment she first saw him and when he swept her into his arms and said that she was his.

How could any girl, unsophisticated and innocent, have resisted the *Marques* Juan?

"Perhaps *Madame* will drive out and see the Palace," the Manager was suggesting. "It is even more impressive than it was in the past. The new *Marques* has spent a great deal of money on it, and the gardens are unique in their beauty."

The *Duchesse* drew in her breath.

How could she ever forget the gardens, with the stone fountains throwing their water iridescent in the sunshine up towards the sky?

She remembered the scent of camellias, white and pink.

They looked, Juan had told her, as if the gods had made them especially as a background for her beauty.

There had been Japanese bridges, rock-gardens, summer-houses and grottos.

He had kissed her in each and every one of them.

They had wandered in the sunshine into the hot-houses and he had picked her orchids.

He said as he did so that they were not as beautiful as she was.

Yes — she remembered the Palace da Azul, with its Gothic turrets, Arab minarets, Renaissance cupolas and gazebos.

She had called it a Fairy Palace.

How could Juan be anything but a Fairy-Tale Prince?

Never, never would she forget the hot summers when they had been together there.

Only when his family came to stay with him

and he filled the Palace with aristocratic guests for the races, was she banished to the house a little way down the hill.

There she was looked after by a number of kind elderly servants until she could be with Juan again.

It had been a dream.

Like a child she had never envisaged the day would come when she would waken to reality.

Juan had taken her to Paris.

He had bought her clothes and jewels that she had never thought to own.

She had gloried in them because they made her more beautiful for him.

They had visited other countries in his yacht.

Looking back the *Duchesse* could remember very little about them.

All she could recall was Juan's lips on hers, Juan's arms around her body, and the ecstasy and rapture when he made her his.

"Yes, *Madame,* you will certainly enjoy seeing the Palace da Azul," the Manager continued. "We have been laughing among ourselves and saying it might have been built for our King, but there is still a King in residence, for how could the *Marques* Alvaro be anything else?"

The *Duchesse* wondered how she could endure any longer this talk of the Palace da Azul.

Then there was an interruption.

A girl came to the side of the Manager and in a low, pleading voice the *Duchesse* heard her say:

"Please, *Senhor,* please, please let me show my

needlework to the ladies staying here."

The Manager made a gesture with his hand as if he would brush her away.

But the girl interposed.

"I beg of you, *Senhor,* to help me, as you have sometimes done before. I am starving and I have no money with which to buy any more material for my work."

The Manager parted his lips as if determined to be rid of her.

Then he found it difficult to refuse the pleading in the girl's eyes.

He recognised the desperate note in her soft, educated voice.

On an impulse, because he was a kindly man, the Manager said to the *Duchesse:*

"I wonder, *Madame,* if you would care to look at the very beautiful needlework that this young woman brings here from time to time. It is, I assure you, of the very highest quality, and not easily obtainable elsewhere in the City."

The *Duchesse,* deep in her thoughts, was about to say she was not interested.

Then she looked at the girl standing a little distance away and realised she was very beautiful.

So beautiful in fact that it passed through her mind that it might have been herself thirty years ago when Juan first saw her.

For a moment she thought that by some unaccountable magic she was looking at her own face.

Then she realised that, although the girl was certainly beautiful, she was different from any Portuguese she had ever seen before.

While she had the dark hair that was so like the pictures of the Madonna in the Cathedral, incredibly her eyes were blue.

For a second the *Duchesse* thought she must be mistaken, but though her eye-lashes were dark, her eyes were unmistakably blue.

It was the deep blue of the Mediterranean.

She had a small, oval face and a little straight nose.

Looking at her the *Duchesse* saw she was undoubtedly speaking the truth when she had said she was starving.

There was no mistaking that the sharpness of her chin was unnatural.

The bones stood out in her wrists above the hand that held the parcel of needlework and was trembling.

"Let me see what you have to sell," she said.

The Manager moved to one side.

The girl came forward and going down on her knees at the *Duchesse*'s feet pulled off the wrapping which was a piece of grey cloth.

Underneath was a nightgown made of silk and appliqued with écru lace.

One glance told the *Duchesse* that the work was exceptional — so exceptional that she said sharply:

"Is this entirely your own work?"

"I was taught at the Convent, *Donna*," the girl

replied, "and the Nuns are noted for their needlework."

"It is certainly beautifully done!" the *Duchesse* said. "I will buy it from you and any other garments you have completed."

The girl gave a little cry and the tears came into her eyes.

"Thank you . . . thank you . . . you have . . . saved me! I thought when I came . . . here that . . . this was my . . . last chance of . . . living."

"How can you think of dying when you are so young?" the *Duchesse* asked.

As she spoke she remembered the agony and the misery when she had been determined to die.

In a very different way she had been saved at the last moment.

"Life is precious!" she said aloud.

She thought as she spoke she was being hypocritical.

Life had not seemed precious to her when she was this child's age.

In fact death had been infinitely preferable to living without Juan and without love.

"I have two other . . . garments at . . . home," the girl said. "May I fetch them for . . . you, *Donna?*"

The eagerness in her voice made the *Duchesse* smile.

How easy to be kind when one could afford it!

"Excuse me, *Madame*," the Manager intervened, "but your carriage is at the door."

The *Duchesse* rose slowly to her feet.

"See that what this young woman has to sell me is taken up to my Suite," she said, "and pay her what she is asking for it."

She heard the girl draw in her breath.

Then she changed her mind.

"Come with me," she said. "I will take you home, and you can show me what else you have made."

"That is very gracious of you, *Madame*," the Manager said, "and I can assure you that this young woman is completely trustworthy."

"That is what I thought," the *Duchesse* replied.

She moved across the hall and the Manager hurried ahead to open the outer door.

The girl followed.

She was wondering if the *Duchesse* really intended her to travel in her carriage, or perhaps she had misunderstood what the lady said.

The carriage was open and the horses looked fat and well fed.

There was a coachman and a footman on the box.

A porter, wearing the livery of the Grand Hotel, opened the door and helped the *Duchesse* inside.

She seated herself on the back seat and he covered her knees with a light rug.

Then as the girl hesitated the Manager said sharply:

"Go on, girl, get in, and sit opposite *Madame!*"

She obeyed him, looking small and rather frightened as she did so.

"Do you really intend, *Madame,*" the Manager asked, "to take this young woman to her home?"

The way he spoke told the *Duchesse* he was anxious in case it was in an unpleasant part of the City which would offend her.

"That is what I said I would do," she replied.

She turned to the girl.

"Where do you live, child?"

The girl gave an address which the Manager knew was in a poor, but respectable area near the sea.

He repeated what he had heard to the porter who informed the coachman.

The carriage started off.

The *Duchesse* did not speak.

After a moment the girl sitting opposite her said tentatively, addressing her as the Manager had done:

"You are . . . very . . . kind . . . *Madame!*"

"What is your name?"

"Felicita Galvão, *Madame.*"

"And you live with your parents?"

There was a little pause before the girl replied:

"My father . . . died last year . . . and my . . . mother two . . . months ago."

The pain in her voice was unmistakable and the *Duchesse* said:

"Then whom are you living with?"

"The Lodging-house Keeper where my mother and I spent the last six months of her life has been very kind, but I owe her for . . . two month's rent, and the . . . food she has let me . . . have."

The *Duchesse* did not speak, and Felicita went on:

"She is poor . . . and if you had not . . . helped me to-day, I could not have . . . continued to . . . impose upon her."

"And now, when I have paid you, what will you do?" the *Duchesse* asked.

"Go on working, *Madame,* and pray when I have . . . finished what I have made . . . God will help me . . . as He has done to-day."

"It does not sound a very secure way of living."

The girl made a helpless little gesture with her hands.

She said without words that there was nothing else she could do.

Looking at her, the *Duchesse* thought again how lovely she was.

"How old are you?" she enquired.

"Eighteen, *Madame.*"

It was a coincidence.

Felicita was the same age, the *Duchesse* reflected, as she had been when she first saw Juan.

It had been exactly three days after her eighteenth birthday.

She had walked along the beach alone, which she had been forbidden to do.

But there was no one to accompany her at that moment, and she needed the exercise.

She had her dog with her and thought he was more of a protection than the old servants.

They disliked moving from the comfort and

warmth of the kitchens.

Moreover, when her mother and father were away, they considered themselves off duty.

It was a lovely sunny day with a touch of wind in the air.

She had run over the sands.

Because no one was with her she had taken off her shoes and stockings so that she could paddle in the water.

She threw a stick for her dog and he swam out and brought it back.

She was laughing at him, her dark hair curling riotously round her forehead.

Because she had been running, her bonnet had fallen down her back and was hanging by its ribbons.

She threw the stick again as far as she could out to sea.

Barking excitedly her dog dashed after it.

It was then she was aware that a man had pulled in his horse behind her.

She turned round and thought he was an apparition from another world.

No human man could look so exciting, so majestic or so overwhelmingly handsome.

She stared at him, and for some unknown reason she had been unable to look away.

The man rode his horse a little nearer so that he could ask in his deep, compelling voice that was somehow magnetic:

"What is your name?"

"Inès."

"A very pretty name for a very lovely person!"

She had blushed.

She was suddenly aware of her wind-swept hair, her bare feet, and that she was holding her skirts with one hand so that they should not get wet.

"I was playing with my dog," she said unnecessarily.

"So I see, and he is very lucky in his choice of a mistress."

That was the beginning.

Inès had walked with him across the sand, and they had sat talking on a grass covered hillock.

The *Marques* had asked her about herself.

She told him that her parents were away because her father was seeing a firm in Oporto.

He wanted to design the new buildings they were erecting.

"Your father is an Architect?" the *Marques* questioned.

"He has designed several buildings in Lisbon, but at the moment, things are difficult, as I expect you know. People have not the money for the sort of buildings Papa likes creating."

The *Marques* had been interested, at least she thought so.

Then they talked about themselves.

Somehow, although she knew it was something she should not do, she agreed to dine with him later that evening.

It was a candlelit meal of sheer enchantment.

When the *Marques* drove her home in his luxurious carriage, he kissed her.

She had known incredibly that she was in love with the most fascinating man she had ever imagined.

Fascinating was the right word, the *Duchesse* thought.

No one, unless they were made of stone, could have resisted Juan.

"We are here, *Madame*," Felicita said a little nervously.

She broke a silence that had continued for what seemed a long time.

"Yes, of course," the *Duchesse* said. "Now, go and fetch the things you promised to show me. I will wait for you."

Felicita smiled, and it made her look even lovelier than she had before.

"I am half-afraid . . . *Madame*, that you will . . . vanish like . . . Cinderella's . . . coach and her . . . Fairy Godmother!"

"I promise I will not do that," the *Duchesse* replied.

The footman opened the carriage door.

Felicita seemed to fly out of it almost as if she had wings.

She ran up the steps of the shabby house.

The *Duchesse* could sense her excitement as she ran up the narrow stairs vibrating back through the open door.

Felicita felt as she had felt when she had run home the afternoon she had met the *Marques*.

She turned everything out in her bed-room to

find a gown in which she would look lovely for him when they dined.

Juan! Juan! Why did this girl, like Lisbon itself, bring him back so vividly?

It was almost as if he was sitting beside her.

Then she remembered the agony, five years later, when he told her he was to be married.

She recalled how she had awoken that morning, thrilled and excited because to-day he was returning from England.

He had gone there to attend the racing at Royal Ascot.

He had entered his best and most superb horse for the Gold Cup.

She had prayed, as he had asked her to do, that it would win.

She had also prayed that he would not be away for long and when he returned they would be as happy as they had been before he left.

She was waiting for him in the attractive house he had bought for her on the outskirts of Estoril.

He thought that the house near the Palace was too small for the times when he wished to stay with her.

Moreover they had both found it an inconvenience when she had to move in and out from the Palace when he was obliged to entertain visitors.

Instead she now had a comparatively large and very comfortable house with four servants to wait on her.

Her garden was almost as delightful as the one at the Palace.

Before Juan had taken her away from her home he had been most generous to her father.

He employed him as an Architect on his several estates in Portugal.

Therefore at first her parents had shut their eyes to what was happening to their daughter.

They had been shocked and horrified when Inès had been determined to leave them.

Yet there was nothing they could do but accept the inevitable.

Her mother had cried.

At the same time Inès had been aware that they were impressed and overawed by the *Marques.*

They did not feel it was such a disaster as they would have done had it been another man.

While she lived with the *Marques* "in sin", to her he had always been her husband, the man to whom she belonged.

That he was returning home made her feel as excited as she had been the very first time he had become her lover.

"To-night," she told herself as she dressed, "I shall be in his arms and I shall tell him how much I love him and how empty the days have been while we were apart."

"I love him!" she had said to the sunshine and the waves beating on the shore.

"I love him!" she had said as she walked in the garden.

She picked roses which would scent the Drawing-Room and their bed-room.

She wanted everything to be beautiful as a

background for their love.

He had returned, as she had expected, at about six o'clock.

When he came in through the Drawing-Room door she stood still for a moment.

She was staring at him because he was so handsome, and because she loved him so overwhelmingly.

Then she flew into his arms quicker than she could move her feet.

"Juan!"

Her voice was strangled in her throat by her excitement and the pounding in her heart.

His arms went round her, but as he kissed her she knew that something was wrong.

It was not that his lips did not give her the ecstasy which she always experienced when he kissed her.

It was just that she knew the fiery insistence with which she was familiar was no longer there.

"Darling, you are back!" she said.

It was a paean of thankfulness because she felt she had waited for so long without him.

But as she looked up at his eyes she asked, and her voice was frightened:

"W . . . what . . . is wrong?"

He took his arms from her and walked towards the mantelpiece.

He stood with his back to the fireplace in a position she knew so well.

"Why should there be anything wrong?" he asked.

"There . . . is! I know there . . . is!" Inès had said. "Oh, darling, what has . . . happened while you have . . . been away?"

There was a silence — a silence in which she felt she could hear her own heart beating.

"I had not intended to talk about it to-night . . ." the *Marques* said.

"Talk about . . . what?"

". . . But I suppose," he went on as if she had not spoken, "because we have been so close to each other, it would be impossible for either of us to pretend."

Inès had drawn in her breath.

"I . . . I do not . . . know what you are . . . saying."

The *Marques* had smiled, but she felt it was a forced smile as he said in a different tone of voice:

"Let us talk about you. What have you been doing while I have been away?"

"I have been . . . thinking of you, and now I . . . want you to tell me what has . . . happened to make you . . . different."

"What do you mean — different?"

You know . . . what I . . . mean! Oh, Juan, how can you . . . hide anything from . . . me . . . what is it?"

She remembered then how he had drawn in his breath.

It was almost as if he squared his shoulders before he said:

"It is because we have been so close to each

25

other for so long that I must tell you the truth. I could not bear that you should hear it from anybody else."

"The . . . truth about . . . what?"

Inès had felt her voice came from a long distance.

It was almost as if they were already separated, and she was talking to him from another country.

"I am to be married!"

Five words, and her whole world was shattered and collapsed in ruins.

Just five words and they destroyed her . . .

"I have brought them, *Madame!*"

It was the eager little voice of Felicita.

The *Duchesse* woke from her day-dream to see the child had climbed back into the carriage and was again sitting opposite her.

On her lap was a chemise of white satin.

Exquisitely appliquéd with a white lace that was as delicate as the blossom of the trees.

The other garment was a petticoat with a lace inset from hem to knee.

The *Duchesse* was well aware it would have cost an astronomical amount in Paris.

She smiled.

"You know without my telling you, Felicita, that you are a brilliant needlewoman. I will buy not only these garments from you, but anything else you will make for me."

Felicita gave a little cry of sheer joy and clasping her hands together said:

"Thank you . . . thank you . . . *Madame*. How can I . . . tell you how . . . grateful I am?"

She drew in her breath, then she said in a rapt little voice:

"I want to go down on . . . my knees and say my . . . prayers to you as if you were a . . . Saint!"

She gave a little sob and went on:

"Perhaps that is what . . . you are and Mama has . . . sent you when I was so . . . desperate that I thought I must . . . throw myself into . . . the sea."

"How can you think of anything so wicked when you are so beautiful?"

The *Duchesse* did not hear her own voice say the words.

It was the voice of the man who had saved her, the man to whom she owed her life.

"I wish I was beautiful . . . as beautiful as you!" Felicita was saying.

"I am not beautiful now," the *Duchesse* replied, "but I was when I was your age."

Yes, she had been beautiful, not only when she was eighteen.

Even more beautiful when she was twenty-three because she had blossomed like a rose.

It was not only Juan who had told her that.

It had pleased him that they envied him, while she wanted no one's love but his.

"The Prince told me you were the most beautiful woman he had ever seen!" Juan had said one night when they were staying in Paris, "and

I am sure, if I was not here he would have tried to take you from me!"

Inès had laughed.

"No one could do that — no one! I am yours! Yours . . . completely and for all . . . eternity!"

Prophetic words — words that she often thought were written on her heart.

Perhaps it was the price one paid, she thought, for being beautiful.

That she should love one man, and one man alone.

Then when he had left her she was without a heart.

It would never beat again as it had for Juan.

Sometimes she would think she was no longer made of flesh and blood.

She was like a picture on the wall, or a statue carved of marble.

She could smile, she could laugh, she could feel irritated and angry, but the ecstasy that Juan had aroused in her was missing.

So too was the rapture that he had evoked with his kisses.

Gone were the little flames which no other man could light, however hard they might try.

Yet once, the *Duchesse* thought, she had looked like the girl sitting opposite her.

Her whole body had pulsated with the emotions of life that came fundamentally from the heart.

Without meaning to, simply because she was following her own thoughts, she asked:

"Have you ever heard of the *Marques* de Oliveira Vasconles?"

Felicita smiled.

"Yes, of course, *Madame,* everyone in Lisbon has not only heard of him, but talks of him. My landlady says he is the most handsome and the most exciting gentleman in the whole of Portugal."

"She knows him?" the *Duchesse* asked.

"Her niece, who is a very pleasant girl, is a house-maid at the Palace da Azul."

The *Duchesse* could understand then how everything that happened in the Palace was immediately relayed to the maid's family and to her relations.

The Portuguese loved to talk; no one knew that better than she did herself.

They made their aristocrats into heroes, just as in olden times they had worshipped their Kings and Queens.

Because she had to know she asked:

"And what do they say about the present *Marques?*"

"That he is handsome, dashing, and many, many beautiful women are in love with him!"

"He is not married?"

"Oh, no, *Madame,* not at the moment."

"What do you mean by 'not at the moment'?"

"He was married when he was very young. It was an arranged marriage and it was a disaster! The *Marques* and his bride were both very unhappy."

29

"What happened?"

"His wife, they say, against his instructions, took out one of his most spirited horses that was not fully broken. It threw her when taking a high fence, and her neck was broken in the fall!"

"And there were no children of the marriage?"

"No, *Madame,* they had been married for only a few months, and it was said, although perhaps it is untrue, that since they quarrelled so that the Palace rang with the sounds of their angry voices, the *Marques* was glad to be free!"

"And he has never married again?"

"No, *Madame.* When the old *Marques* died it is said that the whole family begged him to marry if only to have an heir, but he has always refused."

"Why does he do that?"

"Because he enjoys himself so much with many ladies rather than one, and also he is very proud."

"What has pride to do with it?" the *Duchesse* asked in surprise.

"My landlady, who hears so much about him, says it is because he thinks no one is good enough for him. In fact, they say in the City that he has looked at all the young women of noble birth and says they are all too plain and too stupid to reign in his Palace."

There was a hint of laughter in Felicita's voice and the *Duchesse* said:

"I can see his difficulties."

She was thinking as she spoke of how Juan had

30

told her when he was to be married, almost apologetically:

"I am engaged to the daughter of the Duke of Cumbria. Her mother was a Royal Princess, and her blood is the equal of mine. You must have been aware, Inès, that sooner or later, I must have an heir to inherit my title and my possessions when I die."

"Her blood is the equal of mine . . ."

The *Duchesse* could hear his voice saying it.

It made her realise for the first time that even though he had loved her, she could never be in his eyes anything but somebody inferior!

Somebody who could not bear his name or his child.

It was then, as she looked across the carriage at Felicita's strange blue eyes that an idea came to her.

An idea of revenge for her lost heart.

Chapter Two

The *Duchesse* sat in silence thinking, until she said:

"I want you, Felicita, to go back to your lodgings and have something to eat. I can see that you have been starving yourself and that is not becoming."

Felicita blushed and said:

"It has . . . been very . . . difficult . . . *Madame*."

"That I can understand," the *Duchesse* replied, "but now you are going to feel rich. I have a plan for you which I will tell you about later. So do as I say, and go back into the house."

She opened her hand-bag as she spoke and took out a large number of Portuguese escudos which she put into Felicita's hands.

She stared at them incredulously. Then she said:

"This is . . . too much, *Madame*."

"That is for the beautiful embroidery you have done, and also for the other things I expect you to do for me later."

"You know . . . I will do . . . anything," Felicita said earnestly.

"That is what I want you to say," the *Duchesse*

approved. "And because I want you to feel strong, well and look very lovely, when you do as I shall ask, you must now eat."

She realised as she spoke it was going to be difficult after Felicita had obviously been hungry for some time for her to eat a great deal. The *Duchesse* said:

"Ask the woman with whom you are lodging to give you the best meal she has, and when I pick you up later this evening, bring all your clothes with you."

"Bring my . . . clothes?" Felicita exclaimed in astonishment.

"I want you to stay with me," the *Duchesse* replied, "and I think it is something you will enjoy. At the same time, you will have to work very hard."

"Oh, *Madame* . . . can it be . . . true?"

The words came from Felicita in a broken little voice and her blue eyes filled with tears.

The *Duchesse* smiled.

"It is true, and things will be very different for you in the future."

"I find it . . . hard to . . . believe," Felicita replied. "I have been so . . . unhappy without . . . Papa and Mama . . . and frightened because . . . I am alone."

She spoke in a low voice that was almost inaudible, but the *Duchesse* heard it.

"All that is over," she said. "Now do as I say, child, and be ready when I call, although it may be a few hours before I come."

Felicita bent forward and kissed the *Duchesse's* hand.

Then with her eyes shining, despite the tears in them, she got out of the carriage.

Once again she ran as if she had wings on her feet into the lodging-house.

The *Duchesse* gave instructions to the footman where she wanted to go.

When he had climbed up beside the coachman on the box, the horses drove off.

They drove first through narrow streets where the pavements were crowded.

Hawkers of Lottery tickets mixed with black street singers with guitars; fruit pedlars with baskets, others who had laid out their goods on the ground.

The fragrance of coffee mingled with the salty breeze.

The flower-sellers round the fountains of Rossino were doing a brisk trade.

Along the sea road the *Duchesse* passed mimosa trees in bloom, hibiscus bushes, trailers of plumbago — the blue of the sun-bleached sky.

Out of Estoril the road rose as it left the simple fishing village of scattered huts and houses.

On its right the cliffs also rose high above the waves sweeping in from the Atlantic.

About a mile outside the village there were trees and open ground lush with green grass.

Then standing by itself, protected by trees,

and yet towering above them, was a house.

As she looked at it the *Duchesse* felt her heart contract.

It was still there!

Somehow she thought it might have fallen into ruins, like her own life.

But it was there, in front of her. The house that Juan had given her, and where they had been so happy together.

The horses drew nearer.

Now she could see the garden bright with flowers, just as it had been when she had walked in it, and waited impatiently for him.

She remembered when he had first bought the house how he had said:

"I shall be with you, my darling, as much as possible. And actually, if I ride fast, it takes me only twenty minutes from the Palace into your arms!"

"That is twenty minutes too long!" Inès had replied.

Then he was kissing her so that she could not protest any further.

The horses drew nearer and it seemed impossible that the house had changed so little.

There was the verandah where she had sat with Juan and looked at the sea.

Above it was her bed-room with its huge 18th century bed, carved exquisitely and gilded.

Whenever she lay in it she felt that she was like a Queen.

And that was what she believed she was —

Queen of Juan's heart, as he was the King of hers.

Because she had not given him a direct order, the coachman drove in through the open gates.

Passing rows of flower-beds he drew up at the front-door.

It was not what the *Duchesse* had intended.

Yet she felt that, having come so far, it would be a mistake to go back without having seen what she wanted to see.

The footman got down from the box.

"You wish me to ring, *Madame?*" he inquired.

There was just a moment's hesitation before the *Duchesse* said:

"Yes."

The man did as he was told.

Far away in the depths of the house the *Duchesse* thought she could hear the bell ring.

There had never been any need for Juan to announce his arrival.

She would be waiting for him there on the verandah, or when it was cold standing at the window.

She would watch for the first sign of him riding towards her.

Then as he was silhouetted against the sea and sky he looked as he had the first time she had seen him and thought he was one of the gods.

The front-door opened and the man who stood there was a servant who was obviously not expecting visitors.

He was in his shirt-sleeves without a tie.

There was a look of consternation on his face when he saw the carriage outside.

The footman obviously asked if the owner was at home.

There was a long-winded reply during which the servant waved his hands to express himself.

The footman came to the side of the carriage.

"The man regrets, *Madame,* that his master is away in Africa. He said he is Dom Nuno Comte da Silva."

"I wish to speak to the man," the *Duchesse* replied.

The footman beckoned the servant who came to the side of the carriage obviously embarrassed by his appearance.

"I hear your master is away in Africa," the *Duchesse* said gently.

"Yes, *Donna,* that is true. He'll not be back for three months."

"That is sad," the *Duchesse* replied. "I wanted to ask him if I could rent this house for a month. I think, as I am *La Duchesse* de Monreuil, he would consider my application."

The man looked surprised, and she said:

"As I have to rest on my doctor's orders, this would be an ideal place, where I would not be disturbed."

She spoke slowly and clearly, so that the man could not misunderstand what she was saying.

Then she added:

"I am prepared to pay a very large rent, so that I shall be comfortable, and I am sure, as you could have plenty of help, you will not find me at all exacting."

There was a slight pause.

She knew by the flicker in the man's eyes that he understood what she was implying.

Then when she was certain he was calculating how useful the money would be, she said:

"I am prepared to pay . . ."

She named a sum in escudos which she knew any man in the same position would find hard to refuse.

Ten minutes later, she had obtained what she required.

She gave the man a sum of money with which to buy food and permission to employ three, if not four, extra servants.

Then she drove back the way she had come.

"You would not like to see any of the house, *Madame?*" the man asked before she left.

"It is exactly what I am looking for," the *Duchesse* replied, "and I am also convinced that your master will have very good taste."

As she left she asked herself if she was mad to step back into the past.

She knew that every room would bring back memories which still seemed to hurt her as much as they had the day she left.

Yet, having set out to lay the ghosts of the past, she was not prepared to give up at the first hurdle.

What was more, the idea that had come to her when she was talking to Felicita outside her lodgings had gradually taken shape in her mind.

It was almost as if she was being compelled to obey an impulse.

It had slumbered within her for so long that now it was stronger than any sense of caution.

"Why am I doing this?" she asked herself.

The horses drove down the hill, and passing through Estoril went on towards the City.

The answer was quite simple and she acknowledged it in all its starkness.

It was to hurt Juan, even beyond the grave.

Why should she not hurt him? When he had left her in the house from which she had just driven away.

She had wanted only to die.

She could remember only too well how, after he had told her he was to be married, she had felt for the moment numb.

It was impossible to think and it was as if he had struck her a blow on the head and her brain had ceased to function.

"It is something I have to do eventually," he said. "Obviously I must have an heir to inherit my title."

She did not move and he went on:

"We have always been frank with each other, Inès, so I can tell you now that when I saw the girl who is to be my wife, she reminded me a little of you. I knew then that it would not be difficult for me eventually to love her."

Every word he spoke was like a dagger being thrust into her breast.

Yet there was still that numb feeling in her head which made it difficult for her to absorb what he was saying.

"You will therefore understand," Juan continued, "that it would be a great mistake and might cause a scandal if we continued being together, as we have been these past years."

He paused for a moment before he said gently:

"They have been years of happiness, Inès, great happiness, as far as I am concerned. But now I must behave with propriety towards my wife, and they must come to an end."

Inès wondered if she was still breathing.

Why she did not fall unconscious at his feet.

"What I have already done," Juan went on, "is to place a large sum of money in your name in the Bank in Lisbon. Actually I thought too of handing over to you the deeds of this house, but I think that would be a mistake."

He hesitated before he said:

"You may find this is a little unkind, but I feel sure you will be happier if you go away from here. We enjoyed Paris, and I know there are a great number of men who would look after you as I have tried to do."

Inès shut her eyes.

How could Juan be saying this to her?

Juan whom she had loved to the point of worship!

Juan, who had filled her life so that no other man could ever replace him!

She knew exactly what he meant when he sug-

40

gested she should go to Paris, and she wanted to scream at the horror of it.

But she had a pride which came from her breeding, even though it was not good enough for Juan.

Her father had been born what the English would call a "gentleman" and her mother a Lady.

It was that pride that prevented her from raging at him.

Worse still from kneeling at his feet and pleading with him to go on loving her.

She would have done anything, committed any crime or suffered any humiliation, rather than lose him.

But she knew it was hopeless.

She knew that if her love could not hold him, then words were wasted.

She stood silent as Juan said:

"I have been afraid to tell you this, Inès, but it has to be said. All I can repeat is that I am deeply grateful for the wonderful years we have been together, and in all sincerity I hope and pray you will find happiness in the future."

It was a set speech, she thought wryly.

He must have thought it out when he was riding from the Palace to see her.

Now as he walked, she thought a little uncomfortably, towards the door he added:

"Take care of yourself and remember I will always help you if you are in any trouble."

She heard the door of the Drawing-Room

close and his footsteps going across the hall.

Every nerve in her body urged her to try to prevent him from leaving.

Then she knew that was what he feared might happen.

Loving him as she did she could read his thoughts.

She was aware that as he rode away on one of his magnificent stallions he would be glad that he had not been involved in a scene.

For a long time she stood where he had left her.

She was forcing herself to try and understand what had happened, to face the future without Juan.

It was then she knew it was something she could not do.

It was impossible to live without Juan, because there was nothing in life but him.

He had taken her away from her parents, her friends and everything that was familiar.

Now every thought in her mind, every breath that she breathed was of him.

He had suggested she should go to Paris.

She knew it was because he did not want her in Portugal while he was living in the Palace da Azul with his wife.

When she thought of it, Paris was a misty place in her mind.

The only thing she could remember was how Juan had made love to her in a house they had rented in the Champs Élysées.

The places they had visited were no more than memories just of him.

The Bois, because they had ridden there together in the morning . . . the Seine because they had stood and watched it flow past . . . the Restaurants . . . the Place Vendome . . . the Madeleine . . .

They were just names, smudges in front of her eyes.

All she could really see was Juan's face and Juan's voice speaking to her.

He had left her some money in the Bank. For what?

Payment for their love which could only be paid in the blood from the wounds he had now inflicted on her.

Payment for her to go away and leave him alone.

It was then she knew that was exactly what she would do.

She would leave him so that he would never be troubled by her again.

She would no longer feel the agony that was beginning to seep through her body.

She was well aware it would intensify and become so completely unbearable that she could not live with it.

She made up her mind, and moving without haste she walked slowly out of the house.

She passed through the garden and over the rough ground which led to the edge of the cliffs.

She had expected Juan to stay to dinner and

she was wearing her prettiest and most expensive evening-gown.

Round her neck was a diamond necklace he had given her.

There were diamonds in her ears and on her wrists.

They were all part of the magnificent jewels with which Juan had enhanced her beauty and expressed his love.

Her high-heeled shoes made it difficult to walk over the ground that had many sandy patches in it.

She reached the edge of the cliffs.

There was a rough path by which she could go down to the beach, but which also led, as it turned and twisted, to a deep gully.

Here the waves of the Atlantic swept over the rocks and splashed their foam high into the air.

It was very beautiful.

Just as the rollers coming in on the horizon were so beautiful that she and Juan had often sat watching them.

He had put his arm around her, and she had pressed her body against his.

While they watched the waves and talked his lips would touch the darkness of her hair.

"Your hair is like silk," he said so often when they were in bed together, "and I have never seen anyone look more lovely."

He would sometimes pull her hair over her face and kiss her through its soft silkiness.

She would make her maid brush it every

morning a hundred times.

Then the electricity in it made it dance as if it had a life of its own.

The sun was now low and would soon be sinking out of sight as dusk fell.

"This is the right time to die," Inès thought, "the moment when my body will be carried away in the wash of the waves, and there will be nothing more to remember."

No more suffering, no more tears.

She had not cried, but she knew the tears would come to-night, to-morrow, and every night for the rest of her life.

"When I am dead, I shall no longer remember him," she told herself, and moved a step nearer to the edge of the cliff.

It was then a man's voice said:

"I think it would be a mistake to do anything so dangerous!"

Because it was so unexpected, and Inès was deep in her thoughts, she gave a little scream.

Instinctively she stepped back.

Then she saw, sitting under the cliff, so that she had not seen him as she approached, there was an old man.

He had white hair and his face was lined.

At the same time, he had a presence about him that was unmistakable.

She could not speak because what she was feeling was too intense, too traumatic for words.

As if he understood he said quietly:

"Come and tell me why you intend to do

45

something wrong and wicked when you are so young and beautiful."

"There is . . . nothing else . . . I can . . . do!"

She was only surprised she could speak, seeing that she had been able to say nothing when Juan said good-bye.

The old man held out his hand.

"Come here!"

Because she was numb with shock and also felt suddenly irresolute, she obeyed him.

She felt his hand take hers and he pulled her down beside him on a flat rock.

It formed a seat with the cliff overhanging above them.

"Now, tell me what is upsetting you," he said very gently.

It was only later that Inès realised that he spoke to her in French and she automatically answered in the same language.

She had been well educated and it was something on which her father had insisted.

She was tri-lingual in Portuguese, French and English.

Now the old man said, and it sounded more complimentary than it would have in Portuguese:

"You are so beautiful, so lovely, that it would be a crime against God Himself if you destroyed anything so perfect as your body."

"My . . . body is . . . unimportant," Inès replied, "but I . . . cannot live . . . without my . . . h . . . heart!'

It was then as she said the words, knowing the truth, that the tears came.

First they ran down her cheeks, then they became a tempest.

She was not even aware that the old man put his arm around her and she was crying against his shoulder.

She cried until finally through sheer exhaustion her tears abated a little and she sagged against him.

"Now tell me," he said, "why you are so unhappy and who has crucified you."

Then as if the dam was broken and she was carried away on the waves bursting through it, she could speak.

She told him, a complete stranger, of her love for Juan.

That because he had loved her, but now never wanted to see her again, there was nothing she could do but die.

"H . . . how can I go on . . . 1 . . . living when there is . . . nothing to live for?" she cried passionately. "How can I . . . eat and sleep . . . laugh and talk . . . if he is not there?"

She paused for breath before she said piteously:

"I am . . . dead already! All I want to do now is to . . . commit my body to the waves!"

"That would be a crime," the old man said. "So I have a suggestion, and I want you to listen to it very carefully."

Because of the way he spoke and because for

the moment she did not think of him as another human being, Inès listened.

It was almost as if he was an Arch angel sent from Heaven to help her.

"I understand," the old man said in his deep voice, "that you cannot live here in the house where you have been so happy, but it would be a mistake for you to go to Paris alone. I am therefore suggesting that you die, as you wish to do, then come with me."

Inès did not understand, and she looked up at him through her wet eye-lashes.

"All that should concern you," he said, "is that to those who know you and especially to Juan — whoever he may be — you will be dead."

"That is . . . what I . . . want."

"And that is what they will think."

She stared at him, and he said:

"You will leave your clothes, your jewellery here, and they will think when they find it that you have done what you intended to do."

His voice was very gentle as he went on:

"But because your beauty must not be destroyed, I will take you away. You must start a new life, which will be quite different, with somebody with whom the memories of the past will not be so agonising as they are now."

Afterwards, Inès was to think that the old man had mesmerised her into doing what he wished.

Her tears had left her so weak that it was even

48

more difficult to think clearly than it had been before.

He told her what to do and it was easier to obey him than to argue.

She took off the expensive gown which she had bought in Paris and in which Juan had said she looked very lovely.

She laid it near the edge of the gully.

She added her jewellery — the diamond necklace, earrings and bracelets, as if thrown carelessly down.

Only when she was completely naked did the old man wrap her in the light cloak he was wearing.

It covered her completely from her neck to her bare feet.

Then he had led her down the twisting path which ended on the beach.

It was where the rocks met the less turbulent part of the sea.

Waiting there was a boat manned by two oarsmen.

On the old man's instructions they lifted Inès into it and she sat in the stern where the old man joined her.

She was hardly aware of what was happening as the oarsmen rowed the boat away from the shore.

Keeping out of the break of the waves, it took them only a short while to reach a large yacht anchored in the harbour of Estoril.

Inès was lifted aboard, feeling she was in a dream.

She heard the old man giving orders to put to sea.

It was as if his voice came from very far away.

Then the darkness seemed to come up from the deck on which she was standing and she knew no more.

Inès came back to consciousness.

She found herself lying in a comfortable bed in what she realised was a cabin in a ship.

The sea was calm, and she could feel the faint throb of the engine.

"Why am I here? What is . . . happening?" she wanted to ask.

Then as she made a helpless movement with her hands, somebody came to her side.

Lifting her head they touched her lips with a glass.

She was not thirsty, but she drank because it was easier to do so than to protest.

Then as whoever had lifted her head put it back again on the pillow she shut her eyes.

She did not want to think; did not want to be conscious; she only wanted to die.

She must have fallen asleep.

When she did wake it was to find it was morning, and she knew that what she had drunk had been a soothing potion.

There was a dryness in her mouth which she recognised as similar to that caused by herbs.

She sometimes took them when it had been impossible to sleep because Juan was not with her.

The sun was shining at the sides of the curtains which covered the port-holes.

The ship was still moving and only as she opened her eyes was she aware that beneath the sheets she was naked.

It was then she remembered; remembered the old man sitting on the side of the gully.

He had told her she could die as far as everybody who knew her was concerned, and yet live a new life.

"He is crazy, and so am I to have listened to him!" she told herself. "Why am I here? What am I doing? I must go back!"

Then the question came clear and unmistakable.

Back to where? Back to whom?

Not to Juan who did not want her and was to marry somebody else.

Not to her parents who would commiserate with her, but who would also say that it was entirely her own fault.

Her mother had pleaded with her not to do anything so outrageous as to listen to Juan.

Her father had warned her that she was taking a step in her life that she would deeply regret in the years to come.

He had been right — of course he had been right!

How could she endure the way they would pity her?

"I am dead . . . I am . . . dead!"

Inès said the words over and over to herself.

51

Now she could see her gown lying at the edge of the gully, her diamonds glittering beside her shoes as she had left them.

"I am . . . dead!"

She shut her eyes and wondered how she could suffocate herself, lose consciousness and die.

If that was impossible, later she could throw herself into the sea.

No one would be able to stop her.

That was the obvious solution: she could drown herself.

Perhaps it would be even easier from the yacht than in the gully.

She had somehow been afraid that if she fell as she had intended, she would have to endure the pain of being battered to pieces by the waves.

Instinctively she shrank from the thought of it.

"Now it will be easier," she said confidently.

Then she was afraid because the cabin door opened . . .

Years later she would sometimes laugh when she remembered how resourceful the old man had been in making her live when she wanted to die.

She was to learn that they had not gone far from Estoril that night.

In fact they had merely moved to Lisbon.

Very early in the morning clothes had been brought for her before she was awake.

As she put on a gown, she found that it fitted

her almost to perfection.

It was as if it had been made to her measurements.

When she was dressed the steward, a middle-aged man with a family, told her his master was waiting for her in the Saloon.

She wanted to ask his master's name.

Then she thought it might sound strange that she should not know it.

Instead she went up the companionway and into a beautifully decorated Saloon.

Sitting in an arm-chair was the old man who had told her to live when she wanted to die.

She walked towards him a little self consciously.

He rose in a way that seemed surprisingly agile for his white hair.

"You are even more beautiful than I remember," he said in French, and kissed her hand.

"I think first," Inès replied, "I should ask your name. It seems strange that I should be your guest without knowing it."

"A guest I am very happy to have aboard," he replied, "and let me introduce myself — I am *Le Duc* de Monreuil."

"And I . . ." Inès began.

He put up his hand.

"No, do not tell me. You do not exist. You must remember that you are dead and the very lovely lady I am entertaining at this moment has no past, but, I hope, a very enjoyable future."

Inès had laughed because she could not help it.

It seemed so absurd, and she could hardly believe this was really happening.

"When you were speaking of yourself yesterday," the *Duc* said, "I learnt that your name was Inès, and that, I think, is a name we might keep because it is so attractive. But to me you are Inès Vental."

He smiled and went on:

"Now I have christened you, and we start from there."

Because the ship was moving Inès had sat down, and said:

"I find it impossible to . . . believe this is . . . happening."

"And I find it impossible to believe that anyone could be so beautiful," the *Duc* replied.

Inès blushed and he went on:

"I am a connoisseur of beauty. I will show you my *Château* in France, and my house in Paris. I have also a Villa in Monte Carlo which I think you will enjoy, as well as being attracted, as all women are, to the green baize tables in the Casino."

The way he spoke made Inès feel as if he was mesmerising her once again, and after a moment she said:

"I wanted to die . . . and although you have . . . given me a . . . new life . . . I think it may be very . . . frightening."

"Not if you are with me," the *Duc* replied.

For the first time the thought flashed through her mind that he was a man.

She looked at him questioningly, her eyes very wide and revealing.

He smiled at her and said:

"My dear, I am very old, and while I can admire you — even worship you mentally — it is impossible for me to be your lover!"

His frankness made Inès feel embarrassed.

She looked away from him, wanting to say that was not what she was thinking.

But it would have been untrue, and the words she would have spoken died away in her throat.

"What I intend to do," the *Duc* said, and she knew he was aware of her thoughts, "is to present you to the world as a beauty without peer; a beauty who is so perfect that men will fall at your feet, and women will envy you!"

Inès laughed not only at his words.

But because he was speaking with a beguiling magnetism that she found hard to resist.

"I am seventy," the *Duc* said, "and I thought I had savoured all the joys of life in one way or another. Then when I saw you, I realised I had found a treasure that was not yet in my collection, but so unusual and unique that I have a new enthusiasm for living."

He smiled at her before he added:

"So you see, I am very grateful to you!"

They sailed away from Portugal, moving South towards the Mediterranean.

Inès found it impossible not to be interested and even excited by the way the *Duc* talked to her.

He was an extremely intelligent, witty and well-read man who had travelled all over the world.

As she was to learn later, his collection of pictures, furniture, Chinese porcelain and Russian Icons was revered by Connoisseurs.

She also would not have been a woman if she had not appreciated the gowns he gave her.

Her jewellery surpassed anything she had ever owned before.

At night when she was alone she cried for Juan like a child who has lost everything that was secure in its small world.

At other times she cried like a woman who wanted him as a man.

She felt all the tortures of hell within her body because he was giving another woman what had been hers and hers alone.

She quickly learned to respect the *Duc,* and found her fondness for him deepening although it was different from anything she had known before.

She tried to be what he wanted her to be.

She discovered it was not really very difficult.

He showed her off proudly wherever they went.

After a year together she had been painted by the most famous artists in France and had sat for the most esteemed sculptors in Rome.

"I have been thinking, Inès," the *Duc* said to her one day, "of something unusual I could give you as a birthday present."

"You have given me so much already," Inès replied, "and I am so very grateful. I could not be so greedy as to ask for more."

She thought as she spoke of the sables, the ermine and other furs she owned.

Of the diamonds and pearls, the ruby necklace which he had given her at Christmas and the bracelets and ear-rings that went with it.

"No, you are to give me nothing more!" she protested. "And I can only say again, thank you, thank you, for what I have already!"

"This gift is different," the *Duc* said, "and what you will receive on your hand is very small."

"If you are trying to make me guess," Inès answered, "quite frankly I have not the slightest idea what you are saying!"

"Very well, I will tell you," the *Duc* replied. "I am asking you, Inès, to become my wife so that you will have my title when, as is inevitable, I shall no longer be able to be with you."

Inès stared at him in astonishment.

She had never for one moment thought of marriage where the *Duc* was concerned.

This was simply because she had learned the hard way from Juan that she was not well-bred enough to be the wife of a *Marques*.

It was impossible that the *Duc* de Monreuil, who was one of the most important aristocrats in

France, would offer her marriage.

"Are . . . you . . . saying . . . ?" she began.

"I am saying that we will be married to-morrow in my private Chapel," the *Duc* replied, "and I have already told my Chaplain to be ready to perform the ceremony!"

Inès had risen from the sofa on which she was sitting and crossed the room to kneel down at his feet.

"I understand what you are offering me," she said, "but are you wise? Is it the right thing for you to do?"

"It is what I want to do," the *Duc* said, "and that is always right where I am concerned!"

He put up his hand to touch her cheek as he said:

"You have made me very happy this past year, and while I hope I can stay with you a little longer, I want to make sure you are provided for and looked after when I am dead."

"But you must not die!" Inès cried.

She was suddenly afraid of being left alone in the world again.

Of having no one to protect her from the men she knew would pursue her very ardently if they did not believe she belonged to the *Duc*.

She had always avoided being touched by anyone or being kissed.

Juan had taken her heart and, as far as she was concerned, her body also belonged to him.

The mere idea of another man making love to her made her feel sick.

As if the *Duc* watching her knew exactly what she was thinking he said quietly:

"Exactly! And that is why, my lovely one, you will be far safer as *La Duchesse* de Monreuil than as a lone woman who is 'fair game', especially when she is as beautiful as you are."

Inès had pressed her hand against his cheek as she said:

"I . . . I am not . . . grand . . . enough."

"No one could be more beautiful, and where beauty is concerned there are no rules of precedence!"

She had laughed as he had meant her to do.

Then, although it seemed utterly incredible, the next night she was *La Duchesse* de Monreuil.

But she slept alone.

Chapter Three

The *Duchesse* drove back to the Grand Hotel and told the Manager that she was leaving.

"That is very regrettable, *Madame,*" he said in consternation.

"I have found a house in which I would like to stay for a few weeks because it is so quiet," the *Duchesse* explained.

As the Manager still looked worried she said:

"I am very grateful to you for the way in which you have looked after me, but now I will inform my maid that I am leaving and when she has packed, will you provide a carriage which will bring her to join me?"

"I will of course do anything that *Madame* wishes," the Manager replied.

The *Duchesse,* having tipped everyone generously, drove back through the town to Felicita's lodgings.

She was not surprised to find the girl waiting anxiously in the doorway.

She knew without being told that she was afraid that after all her benefactor had changed her mind.

When she saw the carriage with two horses

approaching she gave a childish little jump for joy.

She ran down the few steps onto the pavement.

"You have . . . come! You have come . . . *Madame!*" she said as the carriage drew to a standstill.

"I always keep my word," the *Duchesse* said quietly. "I see you have packed your luggage."

"I have very little to bring with me," Felicita explained. "I had to dispose of . . . various things when . . . Mama was . . . ill."

The *Duchesse* knew this meant she had sold anything worth selling.

She had needed the money to buy food for her mother.

The footman put the small trunk on the carriage.

Felicita stepped in and sat on the small seat, as she had before.

"You have had something to eat?" the *Duchesse* enquired.

"I paid my landlady, and she was so grateful that she gave me some of the luncheon she had prepared for her son."

"And you feel better?" the *Duchesse* asked.

"Much, much better, Madame! But above all excited because I am coming with you!"

Now they were driving along the road by the sea that led from Estoril.

The *Duchesse* was aware that Felicita was curious but she did not break the silence.

The girl out of good manners asked no questions.

Once again the *Duchesse* was planning what lay ahead, and the pieces of the puzzle were falling into place.

She had gone to her Suite in the Hotel and had picked up a book bound in red leather.

Embossed with gold it had belonged to the *Duc*.

Because he was interested in Genealogy he had compiled over the years the history of the de Monreuil family.

He had been proud that he could trace his ancestry back to Charlemagne.

He had often shown Inès the book.

Because she was now included among the other *Duchesses* of Monreuil, she forced herself to be interested.

While most of those listed were only names to her.

She had found it difficult to follow how the family spread out, not only over the whole of France, but to nearly every Kingdom and Principality of Europe.

Now she was intent on learning exactly who were most closely related to the *Duc*, until she found what she sought.

His youngest brother, who was now the *Duc*, and had two sons, had settled in French West Africa.

He enjoyed the sun and was also a virtual Ruler over a large territory.

His second brother, she remembered her husband saying, had been a great disappointment.

He had refused to marry the aristocrat chosen for him and instead led a wild life of debauchery.

He scandalised Paris and finally was sent to Brazil where he died in 1873.

The *Duchesse* had not been particularly interested in him.

Especially when she learnt he had taken drugs.

Now she wondered if he had married and saw in her husband's writing:

"After his death three women claimed that he had married them: one a Mexican, one a Chilean, and one English.

All paid off and the whole unpleasantness best forgotten."

This was what the *Duchesse* wanted.

Writing also in pencil, and copying his hand, she added:

"A daughter of the English marriage appeared later. Born in 1872 and christened Felicity Beatrice Jeanne."

It was as if Fate was playing into her hands and directing for her the Tragedy, or Comedy, whichever it might turn out to be.

"Her blood is the equal of mine . . ."

The *Duchesse* could hear Juan's voice saying it.

63

It was repeated in the wash of the waves on the shore.

In the sound of the horses' hoofs as they drove up the hill towards the house which had once been to her a haven of happiness.

"Her blood is the equal of mine . . ."

She wanted to laugh and she knew that was what she would do one day when her plan came into fruit.

The *Duchesse* alighted and walked with dignity up the steps into the hall.

The servant with whom she had negotiated and whose name was Pedro was holding open the door.

He was wearing a livery with silver buttons emblazoned with the crest of the Comte Nuno da Silva.

"Welcome, *Donna,* welcome!" he said bowing.

There were two women dressed as house-maids who curtsied.

The *Duchesse* proceeded into the Drawing-Room which ran the whole length of the front of the house and opened onto a balcony.

It was furnished in a very different way from when she last remembered it, but with good taste.

She appreciated the pictures which were not only valuable but also delightful to look at.

Some flowers had been hastily arranged in vases and they scented the room.

As she looked around Pedro brought in a tray on which there were *petite fours* and an apéritif.

She realised as she sat down that Felicita was waiting for her permission to do so.

"Sit, child," she said, "and I am sure, although you have already eaten, that you will enjoy these delicious morsels which have been prepared for us."

She herself was not hungry, but she forced herself to eat one in order to keep Felicita company.

When Pedro had withdrawn Felicita asked in an awed voice:

"Are you . . . staying here . . . *Madame?*"

"We are both staying," the *Duchesse* replied.

She saw the excitement in Felicita's eyes and added:

"While our things are being unpacked, I want to talk to you very seriously, and I think you will find it to your advantage."

Felicita looked surprised, but her eyes were obediently on the *Duchesse* as she began:

"For reasons I do not wish to talk about, I want you to help me."

"You know . . . I will do . . . anything to help you, *Madame*," Felicita said, "but I . . . hope it . . . will not be . . . too difficult."

There was a touch of fear in her voice.

It told the *Duchesse* she was afraid of failing someone who had been kind to her, and she explained quietly:

"It will not be difficult if you use your intelligence."

She paused.

65

Once again she was thinking of Juan and how they had sat in this very room and talked of so many interesting things.

Her father had developed her mind and so had her education.

But it was Juan who had made her think in a thousand ways she had never thought before.

In the Salons of Paris she had been described as witty, wise and stimulating by every man to whom she talked.

But she had always been aware that it was really Juan who was being complimented, rather than herself.

"Yes," she said aloud, "you will have to be intelligent and do exactly what I tell you to do."

"Of course . . . I will do that . . . *Madame*," Felicita murmured.

"Then what I want you to do," the *Duchesse* said, "is to pretend that you are my late husband's niece."

She heard Felicita draw in her breath in astonishment, and she went on:

"Her name, strangely enough, was Felicity Beatrice Jeanne de Monreuil, and she was half-English."

"What would she . . . say if she knew?" Felicita asked.

"She is dead," the *Duchesse* replied, "and that is why I cannot produce her to meet a certain person, as I wish to do. Instead — he will meet you."

"You do not . . . think he . . . will be . . . suspicious?"

"There is no reason why he should, unless you do something very foolish," the *Duchesse* replied.

She saw the anxiety in Felicita's eyes and went on:

"As the *Duchesse* de Monreuil I am well known in most European countries, and it would be a very brave person who told me that I lied or even was suspicious that I might be doing so."

There was silence. Then Felicita asked:

"I shall be . . . nervous of making mistakes . . . but of course, *Madame,* it would be a very great . . . honour to pretend to be a relation of anybody as . . . distinguished as . . . yourself."

The *Duchesse* smiled.

She liked the grace with which Felicita accepted her suggestion.

Then she said:

"I am glad that you agree, and now all we have to do is to see that you are dressed as befits my niece."

She smiled as she went on:

"We must work very hard to see that as a young Lady of Quality, you behave as would be expected of an aristocrat."

Felicita clasped her hands together.

"Please, *Madame,* help me not to make any . . . mistakes. It would be very . . . humiliating."

"I suggest you start by copying me," the *Duchesse* replied.

As she spoke she remembered how first Juan,

then the *Duc,* had corrected any little mistakes she made involuntarily when she was with them.

It was because, she knew, they wished her to be perfect.

As perfect in what she said and what she did as she was perfect in her appearance.

To the *Duc* she had been the living embodiment of the Greek goddesses.

Because it made him happy she had often posed for him naked.

He had never wanted to touch her, he had only wanted to look at her.

So being naked had not made her shy.

She knew that while she thrilled him it was the same feeling he had for the statues set on plinths in his *Château* in France, and in his house in Paris.

He had found her likeness, too, amongst his pictures.

"I have bought another portrait of you, my beautiful one," he would say when he came back from an auction.

Then the servants would carry in a picture of Venus portrayed by one of the great masters.

It was the *Duc* who had taught her even more about clothes.

The *Marques* had delighted in seeing her exquisitely gowned and commanding the admiration of every other man in the room.

But to the *Duc* clothes were an art.

Like all Frenchmen he was content to sit for hours discussing with Frederick Worth, or some other great Couturier, what suited her best.

She learned how to make her clothes a frame for herself.

While they were striking, she was never over-whelmed by them.

Even now she chose everything she wore so that it softened the ravages of time, concealed the alteration in her figure, and enveloped her with an aura of beauty.

"To-morrow," the *Duchesse* said to Felicita, "the best dress-makers in Lisbon will be coming so that we can choose clothes that will make you look very different from the way you do now."

"Clothes!" Felicita exclaimed. "Oh, *Madame,* I have not had a new gown for years! Although I made myself what I am wearing, I could not af-ford the best material or, for the last year, any materials at all!"

"Forget it," the *Duchesse* said, "forget what you have suffered, what you have been or what has happened in your life."

She spoke firmly as she continued:

"Your real parents are dead, and your father, do not forget, was a Monreuil and your mother was the daughter of an English Duke, but you never met him."

She thought as she spoke that the *Duc* would be angry with her for embellishing the family his-tory.

She was however determined that from the very beginning Felicita would be proud of her 'forebears'.

"You will be an aristocrat — an aristocrat to your fingertips," she continued, "for the blood that flows in your veins is the equal of that of any family in the world!"

There was a sudden bitterness in her tone as she finished:

"In fact you have no superior in France, although perhaps the *Marques* Alvaro de Oliveira Vasconles would not consider himself your inferior."

Unexpectedly Felicita laughed.

"The *Marques* . . . ?" she asked. "But he thinks himself better than anybody in the whole of Portugal! I suspect he also includes France!"

"Then that is why we must disillusion him!"

Felicita looked at her in surprise.

"The *Marques?*"

"I want you to meet him, my child, and it will be very disappointing if he considers you are nothing but dirt beneath his feet."

Felicita laughed again.

"That is exactly what he will think!"

"Not if he believes you to be a de Monreuil!"

Felicita drew in her breath.

"Are you telling me, *Madame,* that I am to pretend to the *Marques?*"

"Of course! " the *Duchesse* replied. "You are — the *Comtesse* Felicity de Monreuil — my niece."

"But . . . why?"

The *Duchesse* answered her in a very different tone.

"You have already promised to do as I ask,"

she said sharply, "and to obey me. You will therefore ask no questions, but 'think yourself' into the part you are to play and let me make this very clear . . ."

She spoke more slowly, and her voice was very impressive as she went on:

"Felicita Galvão is dead — do you understand? She no longer exists, and from this moment I am speaking only to my niece!"

Felicita realised she had made a mistake and she hung her head and murmured:

"Yes . . . *Madame* . . . I understand."

"Very well," the *Duchesse* said. "You will call me *Tante* Inès, and as I am your aunt and you are one of the family, there is no need for us to be anything but at ease with each other."

"Yes . . . *Madame.*"

The *Duchesse* rose to her feet.

"Because it has been a long day and I am tired, I intend to have dinner in bed. You will eat alone in the Dining-Room, waited on by the servants, but of course without chattering to them. After that, you too will go to bed."

"Yes . . . *Madame.*"

The *Duchesse* walked across the room.

As Felicita hurried to open the door for her, she put her hand on the girl's arm.

"We will enjoy ourselves, you and I," she said softly.

Then she saw the quick tears come into Felicita's blue eyes.

When the *Duchesse* had gone, she stood for a

moment as if indecisive, before she went to the French window which opened onto the verandah.

She looked out.

Staring at the sea that had become more tempestuous as the afternoon drew to its close.

Now there was a wind driving the waves to beat against the rocks.

She could see the spray shining iridescently in the last rays of the setting sun.

It was however at the same time frightening.

She felt as if it echoed what was in her own heart.

How could this have happened so unexpectedly?

How could she have known or guessed it when she woke up this morning?

She had thought that unless she could sell her last three pieces of needlework she might have to drown herself rather than suffer a slow death by starvation.

That she was already having so little food had made her feel weak.

It also had affected her eyes so that it was hard to sew as easily as she had been able to do before.

She asked herself again and again how things had come to such a pass.

It was quite easily explainable.

Her father's books of poems, beautiful though they were, did not sell.

Her father, as her mother had often said, had his way of giving expression to beauty as other men painted it on canvas, or composed it into music.

Felicita knew that what he wrote was even lovelier than the poetry of the most acclaimed poets of Portugal.

There were quite a number of them, because her father, ever since she was small, had made her read their poems aloud to him.

"You have to learn to listen to the melody in their words," he had said, "then instinctively you too will talk with beauty."

Felicita thought her father had given her beauty in a thousand different ways.

He had made her understand why her mother had loved him so much.

Why the fact that they were very poor was unimportant.

What had really mattered was that there were too many poets in Portugal.

While the Portuguese admired their talent, they did not buy their books.

Although they had little money this had never troubled Felicita, despite the fact that she had to economise.

But her mother had often sighed because she could not afford the delicious food that her father enjoyed.

Then when first her father died the little money he made from his books died with him.

They existed, Felicita found, on the allowance her mother received monthly.

Then her mother died too, and she found herself completely penniless except for what she could earn by her needlework.

At first she managed to sell the beautiful *lingerie* she made to visitors who came to the important Hotels in Lisbon.

Then the shop-keepers complained.

Pedlars, as they called them, were taking away their customers.

This meant that one after the other the Hotels refused Felicita admittance to their guests.

Only the Manager of the Grand would sometimes listen to her pleas, because he was a kindly man.

He had lost his own daughter during a typhoid epidemic several years earlier.

Even so, the guests at the Grand Hotel were usually too old to be interested in attractive *lingerie*.

When Felicita had gone to the Hotel this morning, she had been desperate.

It was her last chance.

"It would be better to die," she thought, "than to live as I am now, afraid, and with this continually gnawing pain within me because I am so hungry."

Then, like a miracle, everything had changed.

She knew it must have been her mother who had saved her at what seemed almost to be the last moment.

"Thank you . . . Mama, thank . . . you!" she said now as she looked out to sea.

She felt almost as if her mother was beside

her as she went on:

"The *Duchesse* is so kind! At the same time, I am a little afraid, in case I fail her in what I have to do. Is it wrong Mama, to pretend to be another person?"

There was no answer to this.

Except that Felicita saw the sun as it set send a crimson light over the waves.

The brilliance of it was there for only a moment.

Yet she felt that it was a message that everything would be all right.

She turned to go back into the Drawing-Room with a little smile on her lips.

Upstairs, it seemed unbelievable to the *Duchesse*.

She had bathed and was now lying against the silk pillows in the big bed with its velvet curtains falling from the ceiling.

It was as if she had stepped back into the past.

It was in this room that Juan had carried her into a Paradise where there was only themselves and an ecstasy beyond words.

As they had lain together in bed she could hear the waves in the distance.

Often they would draw back the curtains so that they could look up at the stars.

"You are the only star in my life," Juan had said, "and now you will shine only for me, for I hold you in my heart."

It was the sort of thing which made her want to cry with happiness.

She thought of herself as a star leading him, guiding him, perhaps inspiring him.

His whole life would be richer because she was with him.

And yet it had only been a dream.

When she woke to reality she was alone and Juan had no further use for her.

Even now, after all these years, the agony was still with her.

Savagely she asked herself how she could have been so foolish as to come back.

Not only to the country to which Juan had belonged, but to the very house in which they had lived together.

Then she knew it was all part of a plan thought out not by herself, but by Fate.

As the sins of the fathers are visited upon the children, Juan's son should pay the debt his father owed her.

It was not that she hated Juan.

What she felt was far too poignant for hatred.

In fact she still loved him, loved him overwhelmingly, as she had when they had been together.

She knew that if he had asked her to die for his sake, she would have been willing to do so.

But that was very different from dying because she could not live without him.

When she had intended to throw herself into the sea, it had been an act of complete and utter despair.

There was in it no animosity or hatred towards him.

Yet now, when she had come back to 'lay his ghost', she had decided that his son should suffer just a little what she had suffered all these years.

When she looked back she had to admit that she had been exceedingly lucky in being saved from destruction by the *Duc*.

He had brought a great deal of interest and, if she was honest, enjoyment into her life.

Even though the one thing he could not give her was love.

Of course there had been men to offer her love.

Especially after the *Duc* died and she was alone.

She was still a beautiful woman and very rich with a house in France which was hers for her lifetime.

She also had a Villa in Monacco which he had given her, again for as long as she lived.

She was rich enough to go anywhere in the world — London, Vienna, Rome — all the places that she had been to with the *Duc*.

She was aware she would be fêted and entertained as if she was Royalty.

There had been men who were attracted by her beauty.

Besides the aura of luxury that surrounded her.

They had been quite genuinely ready to lay their hearts at her feet.

Eventually she had succumbed just once or twice to their pleading and taken them as a lover.

77

It had been from her point of view a dismal failure.

Something within her had either shrunk in horror or else resisted violently another man touching what belonged to Juan.

It was not the men's fault that her only reaction to their love-making was a repugnance she found it hard to hide.

She was aware that she was known as 'The Icicle'.

She smiled bitterly at the thought of it.

She remembered the flames that leapt within her when Juan had ignited them.

She could hear the soft cries on the night air when he made her his.

She could remember too how when he was away her whole body burned with desire until he returned.

"Why have I come back?" the *Duchesse* asked herself in the darkness. "Why? Why? Why?"

Then she thought of Juan's son in the Palace da Azul.

She knew that she must go there, she must see him and make sure that he was like his father.

If he was, he would pay the price for it.

A price that was only a fraction of what she had paid over the years for losing her heart.

Felicita woke early as she always did.

Because she was so excited she jumped out of bed to stand at the window looking out at the sea.

Last night it seemed very strange when she had sat alone in the luxurious Dining-Room.

She had been waited on by Pedro and the young footmen engaged to help him.

The dinner had been delicious.

Yet after the first two courses Felicita, having eaten so little for so long, found it virtually impossible to eat any more.

There had been a golden wine for her to drink.

When she had finished and left the Dining-Room it was apologetically.

She felt the Chef would be disappointed that the last two dishes had been sent away untouched.

She was tired and she had gone upstairs to her bed-room.

Like the *Duchesse*'s, it looked over the sea.

It was furnished with the inlaid furniture of which the Portuguese were masters.

It contained several pictures that Felicita thought should be in one of the Art Galleries.

She was however too tired to appreciate anything but the softness of her mattress.

She fell asleep while she was still thanking God that she was no longer hungry and alone.

This morning she had explored the garden.

She had then walked quickly to the edge of the cliffs to see the sun dancing on the waves before Pedro told her that breakfast was ready.

She was not surprised that she again ate alone.

She was sure that the *Duchesse* would not want to rise early.

She finished an omelette that was delicious and ate a *croissant* warm from the oven.

The *Duchesse*'s lady's-maid came to the door.

"*Madame La Duchesse* wishes to see you, *M'mselle.*"

Felicita jumped up eagerly.

As last night she had not met the *Duchesse*'s lady's-maid, she held out her hand as she said:

"*Bonjour!* I know that you look after . . . my Aunt."

It was difficult to say the words and she blushed as she did so.

At the same time, she had the feeling it was what the *Duchesse* would have expected.

"That's right, *M'mselle*," the maid replied. "I've been with *Madame* for fifteen years, and I don't think she could do without me."

"I am sure that would be impossible!" Felicita smiled.

She hurried up the stairs ahead of the maid to the *Duchesse*'s bed-room.

She found her sitting up in bed, already rouged and powdered and wearing a pink dressing jacket trimmed with priceless Valenciennes lace.

"Good-morning, Felicita!" the *Duchesse* said when she came into the room. "You slept well?"

Felicita curtsied before she said:

"Very well, thank you, Aunt Inès, and I have just eaten a big breakfast!"

She saw the approval in the *Duchesse*'s eyes before she replied:

"That is good! Now Pedro tells me that the dressmakers are here and we must start dressing you as befits my niece."

As she spoke Pedro ushered into the room two middle-aged Portuguese women.

From the glint in their eyes it was obvious they were expecting a large order from anyone as important as the *Duchesse*.

They were not disappointed.

Two hours later Felicita had tried on a number of gowns.

Some were too big for her and had to be altered.

Others met the *Duchesse*'s approval and she could wear immediately.

An order for a dozen others sent the dressmakers back to Lisbon in a hurry.

There was extra money if their workers could provide what was required within forty-eight hours.

"It is impossible, *Madame!*" one dressmaker had exclaimed.

Then before the *Duchesse* could speak she had added quickly:

"No, no, it *is* possible, and somehow it will be done!"

When the women had gone Felicita said:

"How can I thank you? How can I tell you what it means to have such beautiful clothes to wear?"

"Remember, they are only a frame for your own beauty," the *Duchesse* said.

She knew she was quoting the *Duc*.

She was saying what he had said to her many years ago and which she had never forgotten.

"What is important," she went on, "is the picture itself — and that is you!"

"What do you want me to do?" Felicita asked.

"After luncheon," the *Duchesse* said, "we are calling at the Palace da Azul and the *Marques* Alvaro."

She saw Felicita's eyes widen in surprise, and she added:

"His father was a friend of mine — a great friend!"

It was strange, but she thought as she spoke that she heard Juan laugh.

The carriage, which was the same one the *Duchesse* had hired the day before, carried them up the steep road which led to the Palace da Azul.

Perched on a hill it overlooked the countryside for many miles.

All the time they were driving towards it the *Duchesse* was vividly aware of the beauty of its turrets and towers silhouetted against the sunlit sky.

She thought of how often she had travelled this way before.

She had been impatient because the horses could not go quicker.

Her one idea had been to reach Juan, who would be waiting for her.

Because the Palace was so high it was some-times enveloped in cloud.

She thought of it being in the Paradise to which Juan had taken her.

When she arrived she would be shown into the room where he was waiting for her.

As she looked at him she would think he was not a man, but a god.

The moment they were alone, she would run to him and he would put his arms around her and kiss her.

Kiss her until the huge room with its pillars, its marble mantelpiece, its polished floor and chan-deliers swung round them.

He would draw her to the window and they would look out at the view — the green trees sloping down to the valley and beyond it the sea.

It was then she thought that she and Juan were far above the ordinary difficulties and miseries of other people.

Their happiness was so perfect that it was theirs for ever.

The *Duchesse* was aware that Felicita, looking very different from the way she had yesterday, was now looking at the Palace with wide eyes.

The sun was shining on the Arab minarets and the green cupolas.

"It might have stepped out of a Fairy Story!" she said in an awed voice.

It was what the *Duchesse* had always thought herself.

Now she was seeing it again, with its gardens

brilliant with blossom.

The ancient stone fountains she knew so well were playing amid the maze of traditional box-hedges.

She felt for one second as if she had come home.

Then bitterly she remembered the truth — her blood had not been good enough to entitle her to live here!

She had only been able to creep in like a thief in the night.

To leave as stealthily, in case anyone who mattered should see her.

She had been, although she had not even realised it, something slightly shaming.

To be hidden away and ignored except when it pleased her "Lord and Master."

That, she thought, was what Juan had been.

The Palace was a perfect background for him.

It was strange and unpredictable; a mixture of different cultures, different civilizations, different affections.

The carriage drew to a standstill beside the door.

Two footmen rolled down a red carpet and a Senior Servant came to the door of the carriage.

"I am *La Duchesse* de Monreuil, and I wish, if it is possible, to see the *Marques* Alvaro."

The servant bowed.

"I'll enquire, *Madame*, if my Master's available."

Felicita's eyes were on the fountains.

As the *Duchesse* looked at her she knew it would be impossible for any young girl to look more lovely.

She was wearing one of the gowns she had bought for her that morning.

Of soft blue silk, the colour of Felicita's eyes. it was simple, a young girl's gown.

Yet it clung to her figure, revealing that she was, with the soft curves of her body, very nearly a woman.

The hat which encircled her dark hair like a halo was trimmed with a few musk roses.

The colour seemed to accentuate the whiteness of Felicita's skin which was as unusual in a Portuguese as her blue eyes.

A man would be blind, the *Duchesse* thought, if he saw her without being aware that she was unique.

The servant returned.

"My Master would be honoured if *Madame La Duchesse* would join him."

The *Duchesse* stepped out of the carriage and Felicita followed her.

They walked through the front-door into an enormous hall.

There were stone statues and a staircase, carved and gilded, sweeping up to the next floor.

They crossed the hall while two footmen opened the double doors of the Salon.

The *Duchesse* wanted to shut her eyes.

How well she knew what she would see.

The long, exquisitely proportioned room, with

windows that opened out onto a terrace from which the view was a sheer delight.

But first there were the great chandeliers, just as she remembered them, and inlaid furniture.

The pictures had been handed down for generations.

There was the carved mantelpiece in front of which a man was standing.

For one second it was impossible to move.

It was Juan who stood there! Juan, just as she remembered him.

Then as he walked towards her, her feet without the impetus of her will moved towards him.

"This is an unexpected pleasure, *Madame!*" he said in a voice that was so like Juan's that she could hardly bear to listen to it. "I saw you in the distance when I was last in Paris, but I had no idea that you were now in Portugal and at last I should have the pleasure of meeting you."

"You are very gracious," the *Duchesse* said. "You may not be aware of it, but I knew your father, and I wanted my niece, *La Comtesse* Felicity de Monreuil, to see what I have often described to her as your 'Palace in the Clouds'!"

The *Marques* laughed.

"That is a very good description of it!"

He put out his hand towards Felicita.

The *Duchesse* saw with satisfaction the look of astonishment in his eyes.

Chapter Four

To Felicita the Palace was an enchantment that she had never imagined even in her dreams.

The pictures were what she had always longed to see.

But more than the treasures which filled every room there was an atmosphere.

It seemed to vibrate through her and make her feel more excited than she had ever been before.

The *Duchesse* had persuaded the *Marques* to take them round the Palace.

Felicita was very perceptive.

As they looked around she was aware that in some strange way she did not understand the *Duchesse* was suffering in every room they visited.

The *Marques* said almost apologetically:

"I am sure you have seen enough."

Yet the *Duchesse* insisted they should go further and see more.

Finally they stepped out into the garden bathed in sunshine.

Felicita was aware that the *Duchesse* drew a deep breath.

It was almost as if she was finding it hard to

breathe and was gasping for life itself.

She did not know how she knew this.

She just thought of it with a perception which had been hers for many years.

Her father had cultivated it in her when he read her his poems and made her read aloud those of Portugal's greatest poet — Luis Vaz de Camões.

There was not only what she saw on the walls, the tables, and the Palace itself, but there was also the *Marques*.

Never had she imagined that a man could look so attractive, so handsome and so masculine.

She did not express it like that to herself.

She only felt he was full of life and light, and that she was vividly aware of him.

Finally, when they returned to the Salon in which they had first met, the *Marques* asked:

"Is this as you remember it, *Duchesse?*"

"Yes — just as I remember it!" the *Duchesse* said simply.

The *Marques* raised his eye-brows as if he was surprised, but he said nothing.

Only Felicita knew that he had expected the *Duchesse* to exclaim over the alterations he had made.

To mention the furniture and pictures he had added since his father's death.

He had pointed them out as they went round.

Felicita had the idea that the *Duchesse* was not listening, but had stepped back into the past.

In the meantime, afternoon tea had been laid

in the Salon and the *Marques* said with a smile:

"Although I am sure, *Madame,* that being French you do not take tea, you must remember I had an English mother."

The *Duchesse* laughed.

"And the English cannot do without their afternoon tea!"

"Exactly!" the *Marques* agreed. "So I was brought up to enjoy it."

Felicita parted her lips as if to say something.

Then, as if she thought it would be indiscreet she was silent.

"Do you enjoy your tea, *Comtesse?*" the *Marques* enquired.

Felicita was about to say that being Portuguese she more often drank coffee.

She remembered with a little start that she was supposed to be French.

She therefore smiled and said:

"I am greedy enough to ask if I may have another of those delicious cakes."

"But, of course!" the *Marques* agreed. "They are what I used to enjoy myself when I was young."

He rose to offer Felicita the cakes she had requested.

Then he sat down closer to her than he had been before.

"Tell me about yourself," he said, "and if you are enjoying my country."

"I think . . . it is very . . . beautiful."

"As you are yourself!"

89

Because the compliment was such a surprise, Felicita looked hastily at the *Duchesse*.

Was she annoyed or shocked that the *Marques* should speak to her in such a way?

She saw however that the *Duchesse* had risen from the tea-table.

She had moved a little way down the room to where there was a picture by Portugal's greatest painter — Gonçalvet, which she was examining closely.

As if the *Marques* realised he could not be overheard he said insistently:

"When you came into the room I felt I must be dreaming, and that you were not real but one of the nymphs or goddesses who the people in the valley believe live in my Palace."

Felicita laughed and said:

"I wish . . . that was . . . true!"

"Why?"

"Because," she replied, "if one was a goddess, one would have no more humdrum and banal worries, like what one should eat or where one should sleep."

"I suppose that is true," the *Marques* agreed. "You would be supplied with ambrosia and nectar, and I am sure that the fields on Olympus are very soft, although not, I claim, more comfortable than my beds in the Palace."

"You are very fortunate to have such an unusual and exciting Palace. Do you live here all the year round?"

"A great deal of the time," the *Marques* answered, "as I have my horses in training, and a large estate which needs looking after. But I also travel."

He saw Felicita's eyes light up and he said:

"Is that what you enjoy doing?"

"It is what I would enjoy, if I had the chance."

"Then you must certainly go to Greece," the *Marques* said, "and I can think of many other places in the world that it would be a delight to show you because they would be as beautiful as you."

He was speaking in a very deep voice.

Because the expression in his eyes made her feel shy, Felicita blushed and looked away from him.

"You are very young," he said as if he spoke to himself, "and a great many men must have told you far more eloquently than I can that your eyes are incredible."

Now Felicita was aware that she should not be listening to him.

Looking at the *Duchesse* who had moved even further down the Salon, she said hastily:

"I think I . . . must join . . . my aunt."

She would have risen to her feet if the *Marques* had not laid his hand on her arm.

He just touched her.

Yet she had a strange feeling, as if a streak of lightning came from his fingers.

"I want to talk to you," he said, "I want to know a great deal about you! When can I see you again?"

91

"I have no . . . idea," Felicita replied. "You . . . must ask . . . my aunt."

"But you would like to see me?" the *Marques* persisted.

She turned her face towards him and her blue eyes met his grey ones.

Then she looked away.

She did not speak and after a moment the *Marques* said with a little sigh:

"I have no wish to frighten you, so, as you say, I will talk to your aunt."

He rose to his feet, and as he did so, the *Duchesse* walked back towards them.

"Your pictures are delightful!" she said, "I only wish my dear husband could have seen them. He, as you know, had a magnificent collection, but he was never satisfied — he always wanted more!"

"That might be the story of all our lives," the *Marques* smiled, "and because, *Madame*, I wish to see more of you and your charming niece, I hope you will dine with me to-night."

"To-night?" the *Duchesse* repeated as if in surprise.

"I have some friends staying with me who I know will be thrilled to meet you," the *Marques* said, almost as if he was bribing her to accept his invitation.

"In which case," the *Duchesse* replied, "as Felicity and I have no other engagements, we should be delighted to accept yours."

"There is no need for me to tell you how glad I

am," the *Marques* said.

He spoke to the *Duchesse*.

She was aware as he did so that his eyes were on Felicita.

When they were driving down the hill towards the sea and along the palm tree lined road towards Estoril, the *Duchesse* asked:

"Tell me, what did you think of the Palace and, of course, the *Marques*?"

"None of it was real," Felicita answered.

"That is what I thought when I first saw it," the *Duchesse* replied.

How could she ever forget the day Juan had taken her for the first time to his Palace?

She had been awed by the magnificence of it, but cultured enough to know that what it contained was unique.

Yet it had been difficult to think of anything but Juan himself.

As he drew her from picture to picture, explaining who the artist was, and where and when it had been acquired, she was conscious only that he was touching her.

All the afternoon she listened to the tone of his voice rather than to what he had to say.

Although they had met only twice she was already wildly in love with him.

After they had explored the Palace he had asked her to come and stay there.

She had known exactly what he meant.

She had however lied to her mother.

She told her that the *Marques* had a party of friends staying with him and wanted her to join them.

"The *Marques* has asked you to stay?" her mother exclaimed in astonishment. "I have never heard of anyone amongst our friends who has been a visitor to the Palace."

"I would like to go, Mama."

"I am sure you would," her mother had replied, "but I think we should ask your father."

Her father had however been extremely excited by a conversation he had just had with the *Marques*.

He was unconcerned with whether or not Inès stayed at the Palace.

The *Marques* had asked him to design some new stables for his race-horses.

He also wanted his opinion on how a house he had just bought in the Alentejo could be modernised.

"It is the most fortunate thing that could happen to me at the moment," he said, "and from the way the *Marques* spoke, there would be no question of pruning everything down to bedrock for economy's sake."

His voice vibrated with delight as he went on:

"I can definitely develop my ideas on sanitation, which have so far never been accepted by any of my clients."

Inès had known at the back of her mind that her father was being bribed by the *Marques*.

But she had refused to acknowledge it.

All she knew was that she wanted to be with him.

How ecstatically happy she had been those first days at the Palace when Juan made love to her all night.

In the daytime they talked about themselves in the great rooms with a panoramic vista from the windows.

Juan had kissed her in the spray of the fountains, in the hot-houses amongst the orchids.

They had wandered hand-in-hand through the formal gardens.

It has been so wonderful, so rapturous.

If everybody in the world had gone down on their knees and begged her to leave him, she would not have listened.

Her mother's tears did not move her when she said she was moving into the Palace.

The *Marques* could no longer bear to have her leave him.

"I love him, Mama!" she said.

"You realise he will never marry you?" her mother sobbed.

"It is not important."

"It is always important to a woman!" her mother protested.

But she would not listen.

How could she, when she was aware that Juan was waiting for her impatiently.

His carriage and his superb horses were outside to carry her back to him.

It might have been a chariot sent down from Heaven!

She thought as she drove away that the horses' hoofs moving quicker and quicker repeated his name over and over again:

"Juan! Juan! Juan!"

Five years of perfect, blissful happiness, but it had all been an illusion.

A mirage which had vanished completely when she had heard him say just five words:

"I am to be married!"

Five simple words to destroy her utterly and completely.

Although she still breathed, she was dead before he left her.

Suddenly the *Duchesse* was aware that Felicita was looking at her strangely.

"Are you all right, Aunt Inès?" she asked.

With an effort the *Duchesse* came back to the present.

"Yes, I am quite all right," she replied. "I was just wondering which gown you should wear tonight."

"Will it be a big party?"

"Not big, but I should have anticipated that the *Marques* would not be alone."

"Why?" Felicita asked.

"Because men like the *Marques* want always to be amused, and most people are bored with themselves and their own thoughts."

The *Duchesse* spoke bitterly.

She remembered after the *Duc* had taken her

away she had shrunk from being alone.

At first she had been afraid of the nights because then she thought of Juan and could not sleep.

She would tell herself that when he heard of her death he had been sorry and longed to have her back.

Then she would play with the idea of returning to show him that she was still alive.

He would sweep her into his arms and say he could not live without her.

There was no question of his marrying another woman when he needed her.

It was a story which repeated and repeated itself until she could stand it no longer.

She took a sleeping-draught every night so that she would lapse into unconsciousness, and could no longer think of Juan.

It was only when it had begun to affect her looks that the *Duc* prevented her from continuing such a harmful habit.

"I have told you the past is to be forgotten," he said severely, "but I cannot force you to forget unless you try to do so."

Terrified she knew that if she disobeyed him he would have no further use for her.

If he abandoned her she would be utterly and completely lost.

Suddenly she had felt ashamed of herself.

Not because she still loved Juan, but because she was being ungrateful when the *Duc* had given her so much.

She had knelt penitently at his feet and begged for his forgiveness.

"I cannot allow you to damage your beauty," he said, "and perhaps because you have suffered, you have a new loveliness you did not possess before. It is not your thoughts which will damage you, but drugs and drink are a different thing all together."

"I know what . . . you are saying . . . and I am sorry," Inès said.

She had forced herself after that to do what the *Duc* wanted.

She became the woman who had captivated Paris, not only with her looks, but with her mind.

Her parties became famous.

They were attended by all the *Duc's* friends who were famous Statesmen, Politicians, men of letters, and Ambassadors of State from almost every country in Europe.

With the *Duc's* help she arranged that in their house they met the most attractive and the most intelligent women in France.

But the *Duc* always made it clear that there was no one more beautiful than their hostess.

"I have had so much — I should be very grateful," the *Duchesse* thought.

Yet, when she had seen the *Marques* standing in the Salon in the same position as his father had stood, she had known that everything she had attained was worthless.

It had been an agony beyond words to go round the Palace.

To hear the *Marques* Alvaro saying very much the same things that his father had told her about its contents.

His voice was almost identical.

Once again she had been listening to the *Marques*'s voice rather than to what he said.

But she had been aware that, as she expected, the *Marques* had been astonished and intrigued by Felicita's beauty.

He had wished to see her again.

Even quicker than the *Duchesse* had dared to hope he would.

It was almost as if she was writing a Play and seeing the actors behave as she told them to do.

They no longer had any thoughts or feelings of their own.

They were puppets for which she pulled the strings.

"And what gown shall I wear, Aunt Inès?" Felicita asked.

"The most beautiful one you have," the *Duchesse* replied. "First impressions are always important, and every woman looks her best by candlelight."

When they arrived back at the house she sent Felicita to lie down.

In Portugal everybody dines late and the *Marques* was no exception.

There was plenty of time for both the *Duchesse* and Felicita to rest before their baths.

Felicita was unused to doing nothing.

In the past years while they had been so poor

she had sewed every available moment.

Now she found it difficult to lie peacefully in bed.

But she knew that if she was to obey the *Duchesse*'s orders, she must relax and not even read.

It was therefore inevitable that she should think of the Palace and the *Marques*.

She had thought that the *Duchesse*, despite the charming way she talked and moved, had seemed both tense and perturbed.

Felicita knew she was not mistaken.

She had felt a kind of agony vibrating from the *Duchesse*.

She was only surprised that the *Marques* was not aware of it too.

When she thought of him, she felt he could not be real.

No man could be so handsome or, in a way, so frightening, just because he was a man.

She had actually, although it seemed incredible, known very few men.

Certainly not one like the *Marques*.

Her father's friends had mostly been poets and very much older than he was himself.

They had sat talking of their work.

They were so absorbed that, although Felicita and her mother cooked them delicious meals, half the time they had no idea what they were eating.

There had been artists too who had come to the small house in which they lived.

They too had talked of themselves and their work.

While it had been very interesting to listen to them, Felicita had never thought of them as men.

Later when she had been alone after her mother's death, there had been men in the streets.

Instinctively she was afraid of them.

She had however known how to avoid them.

She would wear something concealing over her head and hurry along swiftly to wherever she was going.

When she went to the Hotels to try and sell her needlework, the young porters would sometimes suggest that she should go out with them.

Yet because she looked so young and child-like older men were usually kind.

She was intelligent enough to remain as unobtrusive as possible.

The *Marques* was a revelation.

She had listened to him as she had listened to her father, at the same time being vividly aware that he was a man.

She had felt that he was interested in her.

She saw it in his eyes, heard it in his voice.

She knew, if she was truthful, that she wanted to see him again to-night.

Then as she thought it over, she came to a conclusion.

It was that the *Duchesse*'s interest in her, her kindness, were all somehow connected with the *Marques*.

What was more, the fact that she was supposed to be the *Duchesse*'s niece, was also connected with him.

"Why?" she asked herself. "Why? What can be the reason?"

It was frustrating not to know the answer, yet at the same time intriguing.

When she was dressed, wearing the gown the *Duchesse* had chosen for her, Felicita looked at herself in the mirror.

It was impossible to recognise the shabby, half-starved, frightened creature she had seen in the small cracked mirror of the house in which she had lodged.

She was still very thin.

Yet with her hair done in a fashionable manner, in a gown whose decolletage revealed the whiteness of her skin, she looked like a Princess in a Fairy-Tale.

Her gown, which was white, was embroidered with tiny diamante among its chiffon and lace flounces.

Her waist was so tiny that it might have been spanned by a man's two hands.

Her eyes seemed very blue in contrast to her skin

When she was dressed, the *Duchesse*'s lady's-maid brought her a necklace of perfect pearls.

"*Madame* says you're to wear these to-night," she said, "but to be careful not to lose them!"

"Are they really for me?" Felicita exclaimed in delight.

"They are just what you need, *Donna*," the

Portuguese maid replied who had been attending to her.

"I agree with you, Theresa," Felicita replied, "but I never imagined I would wear anything so beautiful as these!"

She looked again in the mirror, wishing her mother could see her.

Then she went downstairs to find the *Duchesse* looking so magnificent that she could only gasp in astonishment.

The *Duchesse* was wearing a gown which was obviously from Paris.

She was also wearing some of the jewels with which the *Duc* had embellished her beauty.

There was a tiara of sapphires and diamonds, and to match it a necklace, bracelets and earrings.

On her finger was a huge cachalong sapphire which was the size of a pigeon's egg.

"You look wonderful! Wonderful!" Felicita exclaimed.

The *Duchesse* smiled at the spontaneous compliment before she said:

"So do you, my dear! And now we set out to conquer, and who can withstand us?"

They drove back the way they had gone during the afternoon.

Now the stars were coming out overhead and the first moonbeams were glittering on the sea.

It was even more lovely than it had been before.

As they climbed up the hill towards the Palace,

Felicita was half-afraid that it would have vanished.

What she had seen in the afternoon must have been a dream.

But the minarets and cupolas were still there.

As they entered the great hall there were lights, and in the Salon the chatter of voices.

Felicita felt a little pang of disappointment.

If the *Marques* was no longer alone perhaps she would not have the chance of talking to him.

Then as they were announced he walked towards them.

Resplendent in his evening-clothes he looked, she thought, even more attractive than he had before.

She knew he was glad to see her.

As he took her hand in his she felt her heart turn over in her breast.

It was not a very large party of guests.

The women were all very smart, very sophisticated and to Felicita, very beautiful.

The men were all aristocrats, a few of them much older than the *Marques*.

The others either husbands, or else closely connected in some way to the ladies.

There was however one woman who Felicita knew when she was introduced to her was undoubtedly antagonistic.

She was attractive, although not beautiful.

She had the exotic allure that was typical of the French.

Her name was *La Comtesse* de Valmont and

when they were introduced the *Duchesse* said:

"I have often met your charming husband, *Madame*."

"So I have heard," the *Comtesse* replied.

It was obvious that she was not interested.

She looked Felicita up and down almost as if she was trying to find something wrong with her.

She then turned away and slipped her arm through the *Marques*'s.

In a voice that was quite audible she said:

"You always gave me to understand, Alvaro, that you found local people boring."

The *Marques* did not reply.

When dinner was announced he said to the *Duchesse:*

"I hope, *Madame*, I may have the honour of escorting you into dinner."

"I shall be delighted," the *Duchesse* replied, knowing she was entitled to this position.

The *Marques* then said to another distinguished guest:

"I want you, José, to look after the *Comtesse* Felicity as she knows nobody in the party. I can rely on you to see that she enjoys herself."

"It is something I am very willing to do," José replied.

Felicita had already discovered he was a *Baron.*

As they proceeded into dinner, Felicita was aware that the *Comtesse* was angry.

Her dark eyes were flashing as she found herself sitting half-way down the large table in the Baronial Dining-Room.

She thought she should have been seated beside their host.

The Dining-Room was as unique and attractive as the rest of the Palace.

There were statues in alcoves around the room instead of pictures.

The table was lit by huge gold candelabrum and the first course was served on gold plates.

There were orchids of many different species decorating the table.

With the jewels worn by the guests glittering in the candlelight, Felicita thought it would be impossible to be more romantic.

The *Marques* was sitting in a high-backed chair emblazoned with his coat-of-arms.

He looked even more than he had this afternoon as if he had stepped out of a picture-book.

"Tell me about yourself," the *Baron* said to Felicita.

"I would much rather you told me about this party, and who are all these exciting, attractive people," Felicita replied.

The *Baron* laughed.

"I am sure they would feel very complimented to know that is how you see them."

He looked then from Felicita to the *Marques* and said:

"You must be aware that our host chooses his guests as he chooses his food and, of course his treasures, with taste and discrimination."

"That is what everyone should do," Felicita enthused.

"Alas, it is not always easy," the *Baron* said. "We all of us, for one reason or another, have to endure bores and inevitably they spoil occasions which should be nothing but pleasure."

"But, surely, to-night there are no bores here?" Felicita said ingenuously.

"Perhaps not," the *Baron* agreed, "but there are the jealous, the envious and the avaricious, and they are almost as bad."

"I do not want to believe you."

"Believe what?" the *Marques* intervened.

He had been speaking to the *Duchesse*.

Felicita however had the idea that even while he had been doing so, he was listening to what she and the *Baron* were saying.

She turned to look at him with shining eyes.

"The gentleman on my left," she said, "is trying to spoil what is a picture of perfection, like what you showed me this afternoon!"

"How dare he do such a thing!" the *Marques* said. "You must not listen!"

"Because everything is so beautiful, and it is something I have never seen before," Felicita said looking round the table, "I want to believe that everybody is happy."

"And that is what I want you to be," the *Marques* said quietly.

She looked up at him and as her eyes met his she found it difficult to look away.

Then as she did so, she saw the *Comtesse* glaring at her from the other side of the table.

She knew there was one person present who was not happy, and undoubtedly came into the *Baron*'s category of being jealous.

When dinner was over, they moved back into the Salon.

There, to Felicita's delight, there was a small Orchestra playing softly behind a screen of flowers and shrubs.

There were card-tables and one for Baccarat to which the older members of the party were gravitating.

"You are going to play, *Duchesse?*" Felicita heard somebody ask.

"Of course!" the *Duchesse* replied. "How could I resist anything so alluring?"

She moved towards the other end of the room and as she seated herself at the Baccarat table the other places were quickly filled.

Felicita was wondering what she should do when she felt the *Marques*'s hand on her arm.

"I want to show you the view at night," he said.

He did not wait for her to reply, but drew her through a French window onto the terrace.

There was no wind and it was actually quite warm.

Felicita was not thinking of herself, but of the stars overhead and the lights below them.

In a way the panorama was even more beautiful than it had been during the day.

There were several ships moving out to sea,

their lights reflected on the water.

There were the lights of Lisbon in the distance.

Just below them a gleam in some of the cottage windows which looked like jewels in a velvet setting.

It was so lovely that Felicita stood by the stone balustrade looking out.

She felt it was something she would always remember.

Then she was aware that the *Marques* was looking at her and she turned her face towards him saying:

"Thank you for showing me this."

"What does it make you feel?" he asked.

"As if for the moment . . . I was God," she answered, "and I had created the world beneath me . . . and it is perfect, with no suffering and no cruelty."

The *Marques* smiled.

"That is very unusual. I have brought many people here, but no one has ever said that before."

"I am sure it is what you yourself feel."

"How can you think that?"

"I am right, am I not?"

"You are, and I find it strange and almost disturbing that you should either read my thoughts, or know so much about me."

"Now you are laughing at me," Felicita protested. "I would not presume to read your thoughts, and when I told you that was what you yourself felt it just came into my mind."

"And what else do you know about me?" the *Marques* enquired.

Felicita made an expressive little gesture with her hands.

"Nothing . . . except I think you are looking for something that you are . . . afraid you will not find."

She was aware the *Marques* was staring at her in astonishment.

Then he asked:

"Why should you say that?"

There was a sharpness in his voice and Felicita said quickly:

"I . . . I am sorry . . . I did not . . . mean to be . . . rude."

"You are not rude, it is just that you surprised me."

Then in a different voice he asked:

"Who has been talking about me? What has your aunt told you?"

"Nothing," Felicita said. "Nothing at all — that I promise you! It was a . . . mistake for me to . . . say what I thought."

"Now I have frightened you," the *Marques* said, "and that is something I have no wish to do. In fact, I have been looking forward to this evening, and it seemed a long time after you left until you resumed."

Felicita did not answer, she merely looked up at the stars.

After a moment the *Marques* asked in a low voice:

"Did you think of me?"

"Yes . . . of course."

"Why 'of course'?"

"Because . . . I have never met . . . anybody like . . . you before."

"And having done so, what did you think?"

She put her head a little to one side as she considered his question before she replied:

"I thought you were very magnificent . . . very clever and . . . quite unreal."

"Unreal?" the *Marques* questioned.

"I am sure you exist only in a picture or a story-book. In fact as we came up the hill I would not have been surprised if the Palace had no longer been there!"

The *Marques* laughed gently.

"I know exactly what you are saying, and I can understand. At the same time I want you to realise, my beautiful little *Comtesse*, that I am both real, and a man!"

Felicita was suddenly aware that this was true.

Rather nervously she looked back at the window through which they had emerged onto the terrace.

"I . . . I think perhaps I should . . . go back and see if my . . . aunt wants me," she said hesitatingly.

"The *Duchesse* is perfectly happy playing Baccarat," the *Marques* said, "and I cannot allow you to run away."

"I am . . . not!" Felicita retorted, and knew it was untrue.

The moon was growing stronger.

Now she could see his face clearly in the moonlight.

There was also light behind them where the curtains in the Drawing-Room had been left open.

She looked up at him, then looked away again.

"When you left me this afternoon," he said, "it was I who thought I was dreaming, and it was impossible for you to be as beautiful as you appeared to be. Now that I see you again, however, you are even more beautiful!"

There was a depth in his voice that made Felicita quiver.

At the same time, she felt a strange excitement creeping over her.

It was different from anything she had ever known before.

The *Marques* was leaning on the balustrade looking at her.

Now he asked:

"Have you ever been kissed, Felicity?"

"N . . . no . . . of course not!"

He laughed very softly before he said:

"That is what I thought, although when I see how lovely you are, it seems impossible."

"I . . . I would not allow . . . anybody to kiss me . . . unless . . ."

Felicita stopped and the *Marques* added:

". . . unless you loved him. That is what you were going to say, is it not?"

"I . . . I have not . . . thought about it."

"That is untrue."

As he spoke she thought that of course she had thought of being in love, of being kissed, but it all seemed unreal.

These past months when she had been alone, her thoughts had been too engaged on how she could earn money.

How she could afford to buy enough to eat!

How she could stay alive.

There was no room in her mind for love when she was hungry when she went to bed at night.

Even hungrier when she woke up in the morning.

From that existence to where she was at the moment, the transformation was extraordinary.

She found it was impossible to think clearly, or to answer the *Marques*'s questions coherently.

There was silence.

He stared at her little straight nose silhouetted against the darkness and was aware of the tumult within her.

For a long time neither of them spoke.

Then he said very softly:

"I want you to trust me, and, when you do, I will sweep away all that worries you and makes you afraid."

Chapter Five

Felicita awoke early and went downstairs.

The servants hurried to get her breakfast and she knew that she would be alone.

The *Duchesse* had said last night that she was tired and would not be called until late.

Felicita was glad, although it seemed ungrateful, because she did not want to talk.

She thought when they left the Palace that she was in a dream.

She had then dreamt of the *Marques* all night and felt that he was still beside her.

When they came back from the terrace they had listened to the music of the Orchestra.

Somehow even when they were not talking, she felt she could understand the *Marques*'s thoughts.

She felt that he too knew what she was thinking.

She had found it difficult on the way home when the *Duchesse* seemed almost to cross-examine her about what had happened.

"What did you and the *Marques* talk about when you were alone on the terrace?" she asked.

"We talked about the view," Felicita answered evasively.

"And what else?"

"H . . . he said I was . . . beautiful."

She felt as if the words were dragged from her, but she knew the *Duchesse* was pleased.

"And did he say anything else?"

Felicita remembered how much she owed the *Duchesse*. She knew she must answer her questions truthfully.

But she did not wish to say that the *Marques* had asked her to trust him and that he would sweep away her worries.

It was something she was sure he would never do.

Yet it was wonderful to know that he wanted to help her.

But those were feelings she could not share with anyone.

She tried desperately to think of the other things they had discussed.

She could feel as they drove homewards that the *Duchesse,* and it seemed extraordinary, was somehow disappointed.

"I expect we will see him again to-morrow," she said finally when they reached the house.

Felicita did not answer.

She was aware when she said good-night to the *Marques* he had held her hand for longer than was necessary.

The strength of his fingers made her feel as if he protected her.

From what or why, she had no idea.

She only knew that he was like a rock to which she could cling.

That while she did so, nothing could hurt her.

When she got into bed, she wanted to go over and over again everything he had said.

Instead all she could see was his handsome face, his grey eyes looking into hers.

She was aware of the vibrations that came from him and which seemed to join with hers:

"It is just my imagination," she tried to tell herself sensibly.

But she knew it was nothing of the sort.

Now she went from the Dining-Room onto the verandah.

She could see a haze over the sea which was just beginning to disperse.

She could also hear the murmur of the waves.

She thought they were like the music the Orchestra had played last night.

It had made the Palace seem even more enchanted than it was already.

"Perhaps I shall see him to-day," she thought.

It was what she wanted more than anything she could put into words.

Because she felt restless, she went down the steps of the verandah into the garden.

She moved among the bushes which were brilliant with blossom and scented the air.

The *Comte* who owned the house must have spent a great deal of money planting the clusters of camellias, bougainvillaea and hibiscus.

Further away from the house, in a sheltered spot there was a profusion of lilies.

They were so lovely in their white purity that

Felicita felt she wanted to kneel amongst them and pray.

They were the flower of the Virgin Mary.

All Portugal was dedicated in its devotion to the Mother of God.

In the Convent where Felicita had been educated, they had celebrated every Holy Day connected with the Madonna.

She had become so real to Felicita that she talked to Her almost as if she could see Her.

She even felt sometimes that She gave her the answer to her problems.

Now as she looked at the lilies she found herself saying how happy she was to be with the *Duchesse*.

How different the *Marques* was from any man she had ever met or even read about in her books.

He was like one of the Knights who had defended Portugal against her enemies.

Even more than that, when they had stood together on the verandah, she felt he was not a man, but a god.

She talked on and on, not aloud, but in her heart.

Somehow it was not really a surprise when turning round she saw him coming towards her across the green lawn.

She stood without moving.

She had no idea that with the lilies all around her and the mimosa trees beyond, she was a picture of sheer beauty.

The *Marques* reached her.

For a moment they just stood looking at each other.

Then he said:

"You are perfect! So perfect that every time I see you again I expect to be disappointed, only to find that you are even lovelier than you were in my dreams!"

"You . . . dreamt of . . . me?"

The words were only a whisper.

"As I think perhaps you dreamt of me!"

There was no need for her to affirm what he could read in her eyes.

"Why . . . are you . . . here?"

She felt she knew the answer, but she wanted to hear him say it.

"I am playing truant," he said unexpectedly.

"Truant?"

"I told my guests who are leaving this morning that I, unfortunately, could not see them off because I was commanded by King Carlos to come to the Palace."

"And that is where you are going?"

"No, it was untrue. I had a far more important appointment, which was to see you."

He spoke with a note of urgency in his deep voice.

Felicita felt shy and looked away from him down at the lilies.

"That is how you should be painted, and that is how I will have you painted," he said as if he spoke to himself.

Then as if he remembered why he had come he said:

"We are going to do something which I think you will find rather exciting. So come back to the house, get your hat, and bring a coat or a shawl with you."

"Where are we going?"

"I am taking you in my yacht. We are going to cruise along the coast so that you can see my country differently from the way you have seen it so far."

Then he added:

"Even though you are a foreigner, I want you to admire its beauty, as I do."

With difficulty, Felicita prevented herself from saying that she was Portugese.

She loved Portugal, and found everything about it was beautiful and definitely a part of God.

Then she remembered that she was supposed to be French.

The French were very patriotic, which was what the *Marques* expected her to be.

Quickly, half-afraid he might read her thoughts, she said:

"I would love to . . . come with you on . . . your yacht . . . but my aunt is . . . not yet awake."

"That is what I anticipated, and my invitation is for you alone."

Felicita's eyes widened, and she looked at him in surprise.

"Alone? But . . . perhaps Aunt Inès . . . would not . . . approve."

119

"Just for once I am asking you to be daring, adventurous and, if you like, a little rebellious."

He saw Felicita was hesitating and he added:

"I want to talk to you without our being interrupted, and without the feeling that we are being watched."

As he spoke, Felicita remembered the angry glances she had received last night from the *Comtesse.*

She was glad she was leaving to-day with the other guests.

Then as she still hesitated the *Marques* pleaded:

"Please, come with me! I promise you if your aunt is angry with you, I will take all the blame, but we must hurry!"

It was impossible to resist him.

Felicita asked almost as a child might have done: "What . . . shall I . . . do?"

"Come back to the house and I will write a letter to the *Duchesse* saying that I am spiriting you away alone because I did not wish to disturb her."

He paused as if he was thinking it out and continued:

"I will finish up by saying that I am greatly looking forward to entertaining you both at dinner to-night, when my guests will have gone."

He knew Felicita was excited by the idea of going back to the Palace again.

It would be far more thrilling to be alone with the *Marques* than it had been last night when many other people had been present.

"Hurry, hurry!" he said again.

With a little laugh, Felicita ran up the steps to the verandah.

Passing through the Drawing-Room she hurried to her bed-room.

There was no one about.

The *Duchesse* had not been called and there was no chance of her waking for at least two more hours.

Felicita told herself that in the circumstances it was reasonable that she should go with the *Marques*.

At the same time, she was aware that her mother would have expected her to be chaperoned.

"Perhaps . . . the *Duchesse* will be . . . angry," she thought apprehensively.

She took a shady hat down from the shelf in the wardrobe.

Then she had a strange feeling which she could not explain that the *Duchesse* would be pleased.

She had known yesterday when they visited the Palace that the *Duchesse* had wanted the *Marques* to admire her.

What was more she had deliberately drawn his attention to her.

Felicita had felt embarrassed when the *Duchesse* said:

"I want my niece to see the beauty of your Palace because she is not only beautiful outside but also inside, if you know what I mean."

She had laughed as she spoke, but the *Marques* had replied quite seriously:

"I not only know what you mean, *Madame*, but am prepared to believe that she is exactly as you say she is."

The way they were talking about her, as if she was not there, made Felicita feel so shy.

She had not looked at them.

"I am sure you can understand," the *Duchesse* had continued, "that it is a great joy for me to have my niece with me, and also to know that she is my heiress and all the treasures that my husband gave me will be in good hands."

Felicita had heard the *Duchesse* later in the evening tell one of the gentlemen in the party that she was her heiress and he had replied:

"Then she is a very lucky young woman!"

There was a note in his voice that sounded envious.

She wished then, as she wished now, that the *Duchesse* had not tried to make her sound important.

Yet some instinct told her that this was part of her disguise.

Although she could not understand why, it was an essential part.

Then because she was excited and she knew she would find it impossible to refuse to do what the *Marques* asked, she ran down the stairs.

She had with her, as he had suggested, a shawl of exquisitely blended colours to wear in case it was cold at sea.

He was sitting at the secretaire in the Drawing-Room as she entered.

He rose to his feet holding an envelope in one hand while he slipped a folded piece of paper into it with the other.

"You were very quick," he said, "and that is another thing I like about you."

"Are you . . . sure we are not doing . . . anything wrong?" Felicita asked.

"As far as I am concerned, it is everything that is right and everything I want to do," he answered, "and I promise if you have committed any fault I will defend you and take the blame."

"Shall I also . . . write a letter to . . . my aunt?"

Felicita asked the question hesitatingly.

Because he was looking at her it was difficult to think for herself.

She wanted only to please him and do what he wanted.

"Just a few words," he conceded.

She sat down at the desk he had just vacated and wrote:

"Please forgive me if I have done anything of which you do not approve, but the Marques is very persuasive, and I do not know how to refuse him."

She wrote the letter in French and signed her name.

Then she put what she had written quickly into an envelope.

He smiled at her, and walked towards the door to open it for her.

She went down the hall and saw Pedro.

The *Marques* handed him the two notes.

"Give these to the *Duchesse* as soon as she wakes," he said in a voice of authority.

Pedro, who already knew who he was, bowed very respectfully.

Felicita stepped into the open carriage that was waiting outside, and they drove away.

"I . . . I am worried," she said in a very small voice, "in case . . . when Aunt Inès finds that I have . . . gone she thinks it . . . rude and is . . . angry with me."

"I feel she will think neither of those things," the *Marques* said, "and now, for the moment, let us both forget her and think only of ourselves."

"I am thinking of your yacht," Felicta replied. "Is it very large?"

"You shall see for yourself," the *Marques* said, "but I will tell you that I am as proud of it as I am of the pictures in my Palace."

"Then it must be magnificent!" Felicita exclaimed.

He laughed.

It was certainly a very fine vessel.

When they boarded it in the harbour of Estoril, Felicita thought how different it was from the boats in which she had made fishing expeditions with her father.

The *Marques*'s yacht was very large and had been built in the latest and most up to date style.

Felicita learnt later it had only recently come from the ship-builders.

When he showed her round it, she felt he was like a boy with a new toy.

In fact much less awesome and authoritative than he had been yesterday.

She laughed and teased him as if he was the same age as she was herself.

As he had promised, the *Marques* took her down the coast.

Yet somehow it was impossible to notice the cliffs, the beaches, the palm trees and olive groves.

Instead she could only see the *Marques*'s grey eyes, and hear his voice.

She would think how clever she was when she could make him laugh.

Afterwards she found it difficult to remember what they had talked about.

It had seemed completely absorbing as they sat on the deck in comfortable cushioned chairs under the awning.

A steward brought them cooling drinks in long glasses.

Felicita could hardly believe the hours had flashed by when it was time for luncheon.

The food was so delicious that she realised the *Marques* must have a very experienced Chef on board.

The food and the golden wine seemed to intensify her enjoyment.

Because she had never spent a day alone with a

man before, it was to her another experience that was not real.

Once again it was part of the dream in which she had been living ever since the *Duchesse* had rescued her.

After luncheon, when the sun had increased its heat, the *Marques* insisted that she should lie down on one of the soft couches in the Saloon.

"I must explain to you," he said, "that at this time of day, the Portuguese enjoy if it is possible a *siesta*. I have therefore told my Captain to anchor in a quiet bay so that not only we, but also the crew, can rest before we return."

It sounded very luxurious.

When Felicita stretched herself out on the couch with satin cushions behind her head, the *Marques* put a light rug over her legs.

Then he crossed the Saloon to the couch on the other side.

But he sat on it facing the opposite way, so that he could look at her where she was lying.

She realised too that she could look at him, but hoped he would not be aware of it.

What she really wanted was to go on talking to him.

At the back of her mind there was the fear that perhaps she would never have such an opportunity again.

She felt as if every word he uttered was something she should treasure.

It was almost a perfect pearl like those she had worn round her neck last night.

It had been an exciting morning.

Although she did not realise it, she was still weak from the privation she had suffered from lack of proper food.

She fell asleep.

She was dreaming of the *Marques*, dreaming that she was beside him and acutely conscious of him.

It was then that his arms enveloped her and she felt his lips on hers.

It was such an exciting dream that she felt a thrill run through her.

It was as if the sunshine outside had become imprisoned within her breast.

Then as she wanted to go on dreaming, she suddenly realised that she was awake.

The *Marques* was beside her, and his lips were on hers.

For a moment, it did not seem to be true.

Then as his kiss became more insistent, more possessive, she felt her whole body quiver with sensations she had never known.

They were so ecstatic, so rapturous, that she was sure she must have died and this was Heaven.

Then the *Marques* raised his head, and in a voice she had never heard him use before he said:

"My sweet, my darling, how could I imagine there really was somebody like you in the world, and I should find you?"

Felicita looked at him, and drowsy with sleep she murmured:

"Y . . . you . . . kissed me!"

"I could not help kissing you," the *Marques* replied. "It is something I wanted to do ever since I first saw you, and now I know that your lips are as perfect as the rest of you."

He did not wait for her to reply, but kissed her again.

He kissed her until she felt as if she was no longer herself, but part of him.

It was as if she was drowning in a sea of such incredible emotions that it was impossible to think, but only to feel.

Again he raised his head and she whispered:

"I . . . love you!"

She did not mean to say the words, they came from her lips because there was no other way to express what she was feeling.

"And I love you!" the *Marques* said. "Tell me, when did you first know what you felt about me."

"I . . . I suppose . . . really it was . . . when I first saw you," Felicita said. "Was it only . . . yesterday? I feel as if it was . . . years ago!"

"That is because we have been looking for each other since the beginning of time," the *Marques* said, "or rather, I was looking for you, though I was quite certain you did not exist."

"That was . . . why I felt you were . . . searching for . . . something you had not yet . . . found."

"But I have found you now," the *Marques* answered. "I have found you, and I am only desperately afraid that you will fly back to the sky from where you have come, and I shall lose you."

Felicita made a little murmur that was half a laugh and half a sob before she said:

"I do not . . . think any . . . of this is . . . true!"

"It is true! It has to be true!" the *Marques* said insistently.

As he spoke they heard the engines start up beneath them.

As if the sound of them brought them back to reality the *Marques* rose from the side of the couch on which he had been sitting.

Bending forward he kissed Felicita gently and walked across the Saloon.

For a moment she could not bear to think that he had left her.

She wanted to put out her hands and beg him not to go away.

Then the door of the Saloon opened and a steward appeared.

"The Captain's compliments, *Dom* Alvaro," he said to the *Marques*, "but he is proceeding slowly back to Estoril, unless there are any other orders."

"No, tell the Captain to go ahead," the *Marques* answered.

The steward left the Saloon.

Felicita pushed away the silk rug and rose to her feet.

The *Marques* stood watching her, then as the yacht rolled slightly, she staggered and in a second his arms were round her.

"You must be careful of yourself, my precious."

He held her very close against him.

He would have kissed her again, but because she was shy she hid her face against his shoulder.

She could feel his heart beating against her breast.

She knew her own heart was beating with a wild excitement.

It made it hard to think of anything, except that she was close against him.

"I have found you!" he said as if he was convincing himself. "It is true, but people will find it hard to believe that it could happen so quickly!"

She looked up at him questioningly, and he explained:

"I have never before believed in love at first sight. I thought that the writers and poets were talking nonsense! But I fell in love with you as you walked into my Palace."

Felicita would have said something.

But he was kissing her again; kissing her until she could think of nothing but him.

Vaguely, at the back of her mind, she was aware that she was not who he thought she was, but playing a part invented by the *Duchesse*.

She was in fact acting a lie.

Yet it was all so muddled.

As his kisses thrilled her and swept through her body like forked lightning, it was impossible to remember that he would have to know the truth.

As the speed of the yacht increased, they sat down on one of the couches side by side, and the *Marques* said:

"All I want to do is to look at you. There is no need for words or for the questions I suspect are trembling on your lips."

He kissed her forehead before he went on:

"Let us just be happy because we are together, and later the problems which I can see forming in your very expressive eyes can all be resolved."

"You are . . . not to . . . read my thoughts," Felicita said looking away from him.

She knew as she spoke that she was afraid of what he might discover.

She wanted to tell him the truth about herself.

It suddenly struck her that perhaps when she did so he would be horrified.

He thought her so perfect, how could she deceive him?

The mists were clearing and as they did so Felicita was desperately afraid.

She took her hand from his to tidy her hair, and as she did so she said:

"Perhaps my aunt will think it very . . . reprehensible of you to have . . . kissed me . . . when we were alone . . . as we should . . . not have been."

As if the *Marques* understood what she was doing, he laughed.

"You are trying to put back the clock," he said, "but we have defied the conventions and gone too far to start worrying whether it was right or wrong for me to kiss you."

His voice was very moving as he went on:

"But it is right, completely and absolutely right because I love you, and because I know, even if you had not told me so, that you love me too."

"How can you be . . . sure of . . . that?" Felicita asked.

In answer, he took her hand again and turning it over put his lips against her palm.

It was a long, slow, passionate kiss.

Because it was something that had never happened to her before Felicita was at first surprised.

Then as she thrilled to the insistence of his lips, he could see in her eyes what she was feeling.

He knew too that she drew in her breath because it was difficult to breathe.

Her breasts were moving beneath the thin material of her blue gown.

He held her hand in both of his and asked:

"Now tell me what you are feeling and if anything else is of importance."

It was impossible to speak.

She could only look at him until he put his arms around her and pulled her roughly against him.

"You are mine!" he said. "Mine, as you have been since the moment you were born, and Fate has been moving us towards each other until at last we are together."

He kissed her fiercely, as if he would conquer her with his kisses.

Only when she was limp in his arms from the rapture of it, did he say triumphantly:

"Now tell me you love me!"

"I . . . love . . . you . . ."

He kissed her again very gently.

Then to her surprise, because she had not expected it, he took her out on deck.

Now Felicita could see the Palace da Azul silhouetted against the sky.

It looked more fairy-like and even more romantic than it had done yesterday.

There was no need for words.

With the *Marques*'s arms around her, Felicita stood looking at his home.

She knew it was as strange and unpredictable as he was himself.

They both, she thought, stirred the imagination and were too extraordinary to be human.

Only when finally, time having seemed to go by in a flash, they moved into the harbour, did the *Marques* ask:

"Have I made you happy?"

"So . . . happy that there are no words with which to . . . describe it!" Felicita said in a rapt little voice.

"We are in love," the *Marques* said, "and words are always inadequate when what we want to express comes from our hearts."

She wondered how he could understand so exactly what she was feeling.

With a little smile she went back into the Saloon to collect her hat and her shawl.

When they reached the shore the *Marques*'s carriage was waiting for them.

He held her hand as they drove back to the house.

When they stepped out of the carriage Pedro said the *Duchesse* was in the Drawing-Room.

Felicita felt she could not face her.

How could she make the explanations that she knew would have to be made as to why she and the *Marques* had gone away together.

They had spent the day, reprehensibly from a social point of view, alone.

But to speak of it must destroy the magic that still held her spellbound.

She stood irresolute in the hall, and as if he understood what she was feeling, the *Marques* said quietly:

"Go upstairs, my darling, and leave this to me."

Pedro opened the Drawing-Room door for him and as he passed through it Felicita fled up the stairs.

She went into her room.

Pulling off her hat she flung herself down on the bed to hide her face in the pillow.

Everything that had happened seemed utterly and completely incredible.

She was not the same person who had left this room early this morning.

Then she had loved him, but it had been a spiritual love.

As ethereal as the mist over the sea, as pure as the lilies she had found in the garden.

It was a love intense and real.

The same love she gave to the Virgin Mary whom she worshipped and the God in whom she believed.

Now the *Marques*'s lips had awoken her to womanhood.

She loved him not only as a Knight, or a god-like creature without substance, but as a man.

She could feel her whole body vibrating to his.

Although in her innocence she did not understand, she wanted to be a part of him.

She wanted to belong to him as he said she did.

The thrills that ran through her were like little tongues of flame.

"I love . . . him! I . . . love him! I love . . . him!" she said into her pillow.

What she felt for him was so compelling that her brain could not grasp how overwhelming it was.

It seemed a long time later before there was a knock on her door.

Maria, the maid came in.

Quickly Felicita sat up on the bed.

"You rest, *Donna*," Maria said. "There is no hurry."

"No . . . hurry?" Felicita repeated stupidly.

"No *Donna*, you're to be ready to leave for the Palace at eight-thirty, and until then, you should sleep."

135

Felicita drew in her breath.

Obviously the *Duchesse* did not wish to see her.

That meant she was not angry, or she would not have accepted the *Marques*'s invitation for them to go again to the Palace.

With a little smile she told herself he always got his own way.

Somehow he would have persuaded the *Duchesse* that they had done nothing wrong.

Even the *Duchesse,* like every other woman, found him irresistible!

Felicita let Maria help her out of her clothes and into one of the beautiful diaphanous nightgowns.

It was not as well sewn as those she made herself.

But the materials were finer and the lace more expensive than she could afford to buy.

She did not want to think of the work she had done.

Or of the desperate days when she had gone from hotel to hotel trying to find a buyer for her wares.

Instead she got into bed, and thought only of the *Marques.*

She could feel his arms around her, his lips on hers.

She knew she was safe because he was holding her.

There were a thousand problems ahead, waiting to be solved.

She shied away from them like a frightened

horse faced with a fence that was too high for it to jump.

She would not — she dared not — think of what the future held.

There were explanations to be made, apologies offered.

Perhaps retribution would follow then.

If the *Marques* was angry, what could she do about it?

What was more, because she had given her word to the *Duchesse* who had done so much for her, she must continue to be deceitful.

At least until she was released from her vow of allegiance.

"I am sure she will understand when she realises that we are in love with each other," Felicita thought confidently.

Because she was afraid of the answer, she forced herself, and it was not difficult, to think only of the *Marques*.

His lips, his kisses, and him!

Chapter Six

Driving towards the Palace, Felicita was tense with excitement.

She did not realise until they were nearly there that the *Duchesse* was very quiet.

There was a faint smile on her lips.

Yet Felicita had the idea that she was not particularly happy.

It seemed strange, but there was nothing she could put into words.

She could only wonder if, after all, the *Duchesse* was annoyed with her because she had been out all day in the yacht with the *Marques*.

She had waited for the *Duchesse* apprehensively.

She was wearing the gown that she had been informed she was to wear.

The pale translucent blue of a thrush's egg, it was trimmed with snow-drops.

They seemed a little out of place in the warm sunshine.

Yet she knew it made her look very young and at the same time innocent and untouched.

Instinctively she thought of the lilies.

When the *Marques* had arrived this morning

she had been standing amongst them.

For the first time she wondered if perhaps he had been shocked that she had allowed him to kiss her.

But 'allowed' was not the right word.

She had been asleep when his lips found hers.

She could not have struggled or resisted him.

It would have been like standing up against one of the great waves flowing in from the Atlantic and breaking against the rocks.

Her love had seemed then to flow over her like a flood tide.

She knew it had intensified until the idea of seeing him again made her feel breathless.

She had no idea that the *Duchesse* was vividly conscious of the brilliance of her eyes.

Once again the older woman was stepping back into the past.

She was remembering how she felt when she had driven to the Palace to find Juan waiting for her.

The *Marques* had overwhelmed her and she had thought foolishly that their love was as eternal as the sea.

Felicita was not aware that the gown she was wearing was almost a replica of one the *Duchesse* had worn.

It was soon after she met Juan and she had bought it when her mother was not with her.

It cost a great deal more than they usually spent.

She suspected that if she had asked for permission to buy it her mother would have refused.

The colour of the soft material had been a background for the darkness of her hair, the whiteness of her skin and the happiness in her eyes.

The snow-drops, the first flower of Spring, symbolised the blooming of emotions she had not known before.

She would never forget that particular evening, for it was then that Juan had said to her:

"I cannot bear any longer this parting and your leaving me! You must tell your mother to-morrow that you are coming to stay at the Palace."

She had looked at him somewhat apprehensively and he said:

"Say there is a party, say the Queen herself is here to chaperon you, but for God's sake come, or I think I shall go mad without you!"

He had not waited for her reply, but swept her into his arms.

He had kissed her until she agreed to do anything he asked.

It was impossible to think about anything but him and their love.

She knew that was what Felicita was feeling now.

She wondered a little cynically whether, if the *Marques* offered to take her away, she would be strong enough to resist him.

It was impossible to be with Felicita and not be aware how much her religion meant to her.

The teaching of the Nuns, her belief in God and the Virgin Mary, was so much a part of her character and personality.

The *Duchesse* knew in that respect she was different from the girl she had been when Juan first found her.

Her parents were Catholics, but not particularly ardent ones.

She herself had been far too conscious of her own beauty at a very early age to worship the abstract beauty that filled Felicita's eyes.

Now she knew the girl had awoken from being a child into becoming a woman.

Where before she had been concerned only with her soul now she felt all the pulsating emotions of the heart.

The *Duchesse* forced herself not to go on thinking about Felicita.

Instead she thought about her plan and that everything so far had taken place exactly as she wished it to do.

Felicita was in love, and so was the *Marques!*

Her years with the *Duc* had taught her to know when a man was completely sincere or pretending.

She knew too when what was called 'love' was no more than a passing desire for a pretty face and a softly curved body.

Everything was happening very quickly.

Yet she was prepared to wager a great deal of her large fortune that the *Marques* was completely captivated by Felicita.

In fact it was only a question now as to how long it would be before he declared himself.

If it was to-night, she was ready.

The horses turned in at the gates.

They started the last climb up the steep drive to the Palace.

The dying rays of the sun were turning the cupolas and the spiral tops of the minarets to gold.

It was so lovely that the *Duchesse* heard Felicita draw in her breath.

She knew that the girl was once again in a Fairyland where nothing was real.

Everything an enchantment!

As usual, the footmen in their livery rolled down the red carpet.

The Major Domo bowed low and the *Duchesse* swept into the Palace with Felicita behind her.

Two footmen hurried ahead of them to open the double doors into the Salon.

Before they could do so, as if the *Marques* was too impatient to wait, he had pulled them open himself.

He came out of the room to greet the *Duchesse*.

"You know how glad I am to see you!" he said.

She did not miss the note of sincerity in his voice.

He kissed her hand, but as if he could not help himself, his eyes were already on Felicita.

For a moment they just stared at each other, and she forgot to curtsy.

Then as hastily she did so, she could feel his

fingers tighten on hers.

It was with the greatest difficulty that she did not throw herself into his arms.

"Now we can enjoy ourselves," the *Marques* said. "A party always makes it difficult to talk to a person one wants to."

"Nevertheless I enjoyed myself last night," the *Duchesse* smiled.

With the ease of an experienced, sophisticated hostess, she began to talk of the *Marques*'s guests.

She told him amusing little anecdotes of those she had known in the past.

He laughed, as she had expected him to do.

At the same time his eyes kept going towards Felicita.

When she refused a glass of champagne she was offered by one of the flunkeys, he rose.

Taking a glass from the tray, he put it into her hand.

"To-night we celebrate what to me has been a perfect day!" he said.

She realised his eyes were on her lips and he was thinking of how for the first time he had kissed her.

She blushed, but obediently took a tiny sip from the glass.

They went into dinner and she was aware that the *Marques* was not only looking happy, but was really enjoying himself.

He determined that his guests should be happy too.

He told them interesting stories of the Palace,

143

his estate, and the people who worked for him.

He did not make the mistake, as many men might have done, of talking to the *Duchesse* of people they both knew in Paris.

That would have precluded Felicita from the conversation.

Instead his tales were those she could understand, and which he knew she would enjoy.

Some concerned the history of Portugal.

When he spoke of the Knights, he knew from the expression in her eyes that she was thinking of him in shining armour.

The food was even more delicious than it had been the night before.

As if he knew it was what she would enjoy, half-way through the meal an Orchestra, hidden in the Minstrels' Gallery, began to play very softly as a background to what they were saying.

To-night the table was decorated with jewelled vessels of gold.

The *Marques* said they had been in his family for many centuries, and had been made by the greatest craftsmen in the world.

The orchids which decorated the table were all white.

Felicita knew why the *Marques* had chosen them.

When she realised it, she saw there were lilies in great vases on either side of the fireplace.

As she gave him a faint little smile he knew that she was thanking him for thinking of her.

When the servants had withdrawn they sat for

144

quite a long time at the dinner-table.

The soft strains of Strauss's romantic music filled the air.

Then at last they moved from the Dining-Room into the Salon.

Electric light had been introduced in a great number of buildings in Lisbon, but the *Marques* insisted it would spoil the Palace.

The light from the chandeliers and the crystal candelabra standing on some of the tables was soft and certainly beautifying.

There was the fragrance of the flowers and the windows open to the star-strewn night outside.

It made Felicita feel that no background could be more perfect for her love of the *Marques,* or his for her.

As they sat at dinner they had vibrated to each other.

Sometimes in the middle of a sentence he would forget what he was saying.

She knew that it was because he wanted to take her in his arms.

She felt a little thrill run through her because it was what she wanted too.

She wondered if there would be a chance of their being alone together.

Instinctively she moved a little nearer to the window.

She was not aware that the *Duchesse* knew exactly what she was feeling.

She was remembering one evening when she had come from the Dining-Room with Juan.

As they entered the Salon Juan had said:

"I forgot to tell you, my lovely one, that to-morrow I have to go away."

She had given a little cry of protest.

"Oh, no! Why, and where are you going?"

"I have an appointment in Madrid that I cannot avoid. The King of Spain has asked me to discuss a matter of policy with him. I have put him off so often, that I dare not put him off any more."

"But I shall be here alone!" Inès cried.

"Only for two or three days."

"Days will seem like centuries!"

"So you will miss me?"

"You know I shall be miserable and unhappy without you."

"As I shall be without you."

She had walked to the window and out onto the terrace.

She had felt that to move would relieve the pain that Juan was inflicting on her.

It was one of the penalties she paid for giving herself so whole-heartedly into his keeping.

When he was away she made no effort to get in touch with her family or her previous friends.

She did not want them to ask her questions, or pry into what was entirely her secret and intimate life.

When he was not there she was alone.

Alone in the vastness of the Palace that seemed very empty without him.

The garden became a wilderness, and there

was nothing she could do but wait and go on waiting until he returned.

Then Juan had joined her on the terrace.

They had leaned on the balustrade looking at the lights below them.

As if he followed her thoughts, as he was always able to do, he had said, looking down:

"I brought you away from all that. Do you regret living in the clouds, or would you like to go back?"

"How can you ask me such an absurd question? I am happy, utterly and completely happy, but afraid."

"Afraid?" he queried.

"That when you go away I may lose you."

He had laughed and it was a very tender sound.

"That is impossible! I shall be back just as quickly as it is possible for me to do so, and it is only two or perhaps three days out of a lifetime."

The *Duchesse* thought bitterly how a 'lifetime' had been whittled down to five years.

Five years, then he had found her not good enough for him.

He had thrust her away because her blood did not equal that of the high and mighty *Marques* Juan de Oliveira Vasconles.

Even to think of it made her feel again that he had thrust a dagger into her heart.

She had died from the agony of it.

Then she was aware that the *Marques* had joined Felicita at the window.

147

She was looking up at him.

She was thinking perhaps he would take her outside.

Then at last they could speak to each other without the *Duchesse* overhearing what they were saying.

Instead he looked down at her for a long moment.

She felt a little quiver run through her because his eyes were on her lips.

Then with a faint smile he put out his hand and taking hers said:

"What are we waiting for?"

She did not understand.

But she held onto him as he drew her slowly back to where the *Duchesse* was sitting on the sofa watching them.

They came to a standstill in front of her.

"Madame," the *Marques* said, "we have something to tell you, something which I feel actually will not surprise you."

The *Duchesse* looked at him inquiringly and the *Marques* went on:

"We are in love. It may seem to you too soon, but we fell in love the moment we saw each other."

He looked at Felicita and went on:

"It was pre-ordained since the beginning of time that we should meet and I should find what I have been seeking for years, only to be disappointed."

As he spoke, Felicita drew a little nearer to him.

Now he put his arm around her waist.

Impulsively she pressed her cheek against his shoulder.

"You do not surprise me," the *Duchesse* said after what seemed a long silence. "At the same time, what do you intend to do about it?"

"The answer to that question is quite simple," the *Marques* replied. "We wish to be married as soon as you give us permission to do so, in a week, or ten days! I cannot wait any longer!"

Felicita gave a little gasp.

Then realising what he had said she looked at the *Duchesse* pleadingly.

Thoughts were flashing through her mind.

She wondered whether the *Duchesse* would tell him the truth, or would leave him for the moment in ignorance.

Because she was bemused and at the same time thrilled because the *Marques* wanted her, she could not formulate her own opinion.

"Did I hear you correctly?" the *Duchesse* asked quietly.

She spoke, but in a voice that seemed different from the way she spoke ordinarily.

"You wish to marry my niece, and heir?"

"I want her to be my wife," the *Marques* said.

"You are quite certain of that?"

"As I have already said," the *Marques* replied, "it may seem too soon when we have only just met each other. But there is no time where love is concerned, and so, please, *Madame La Duchesse,* be generous and let us be married as quickly as possible!"

He made a gesture with his hand before he went on:

"And where could be more appropriate than here in the Palace in my own Chapel?"

The *Duchesse* put out her hand.

"Come here, Felicita!"

Obediently Felicita moved towards her.

The *Duchesse* drew her down beside her on the sofa while the *Marques* remained standing.

"You have asked me," she said, "to sanction a marriage between you, the *Marques* Alvaro de Oliveira Vasconles, and a girl you know as 'Felicity', whom you tell me you love."

"I love her!" the *Marques* said in his deep voice, "and she loves me!"

"That she loves you I can well believe," the *Duchesse* remarked, "but I doubt if you love her enough . . ."

The *Marques* made a gesture that was very eloquent, and he said:

"I am thirty-two, and have, as you know, been married once, and it was a disaster. I was determined never again to have an arranged marriage, but to find somebody I love and who loves me."

He smiled and it made him look very attractive as he continued:

"That is what I have done, and I consider myself the most fortunate man in the world!"

"Words! Words!" the *Duchesse* said. "Words . . . that I have heard before, and in this very room!"

The *Marques* looked at her with a puzzled expression on his face.

She went on:

"I thought when you met Felicita this was how you would feel about her, and it was what many years ago your father felt for me."

Now the *Marques* was obviously surprised, but he did not speak.

"I was exactly Felicita's age," the *Duchesse* said, "when we met on the sea-shore, and he took me from my family and brought me here to the Palace, and I became his mistress!"

Her voice sharpened as she repeated:

"His mistress!"

Now the *Marques* was staring at her in complete astonishment.

His eyes were on the *Duchesse*'s face.

He was listening to her intently as he sat down automatically in a chair opposite her.

"I had no idea of this!"

"Why should you?" she enquired. "And when after five years your father informed me that he was going to marry somebody whose blood and breeding he considered good enough for him, I died!"

There was a look of bewilderment on the *Marques*'s face and she said:

"I am telling you the truth, although it is difficult to explain. Your father had gone to England, and when he returned he informed me he had become engaged to the woman who was your mother, because she was the daughter of a Duke!"

151

Felicita made a little murmur.

She was quick-witted enough to realise where the *Duchesse*'s story was leading.

She wanted to cry out in horror.

She could not move, could not speak.

She could only stay where she was and listen as the *Duchesse* went on:

"He gave me money and told me to go to Paris where doubtless I would find another man to be my Protector, as he had been!"

There was a sudden agony in her voice as she said:

"I loved him, I had given him my heart! I never thought for one moment that our love was something low and degrading, that I was in reality nothing more to him than a kept woman who could be bought off!"

She almost spat the last words before she said:

"I said I died, and you did not believe me, but that is exactly what I did. I went down to the sea to throw myself to the rocks, but was saved by the *Duc* de Monreuil, who later married me."

Her voice sharpened:

"Although he married my body and my mind, he could not have my heart. Your father had taken that and destroyed it!"

Felicita could feel the pain of what she was saying.

She put out her hand and laid it on her arm as if to comfort her.

The *Duchesse* shook it off.

"All these years," she said, "I have loved only

your father, and although I lived a new life in Paris, he always haunted me. I have never forgotten him, not for one minute of the day or night. He has always been with me!"

For a moment there was a suspicion of tears in her eyes.

Then as if she forced herself to challenge the *Marques* she said:

"That is why I planned my revenge on you — your father's son!"

The *Marques* would have spoken, but she went on quickly:

"I came back to Portugal to lay the ghost, and when I saw Felicita, I knew that Fate had given me a weapon by which I could hurt you as I have been hurt."

"I do not understand . . ." the *Marques* began.

"You will understand," the *Duchesse* interrupted, "when I tell you that Felicita, for that is her real name, is nothing but a Portuguese street pedlar! A girl who came in from the streets, starving and trying to sell her wares in the hall of the Grand Hotel!"

The *Duchesse* laughed, and now the sound seemed to ring round the great room.

"A Portuguese pedlar! Are you sure, my noble *Marques*, that you wish to mix your blue blood of which you are so proud with the scrapings of the gutter?"

Felicita gave a cry of protest.

"They say you have never found anybody good enough to marry," the *Duchesse* went on, "but I hardly think your father, who considered me beneath him, would be pleased at your choice, or that your children, who will inherit your title, would be proud of their mother!"

The *Marques* seemed as if he was turned to stone.

The *Duchesse* rising to her feet pulled Felicita to hers.

"Remember what I have told you," she said, "and if your pride is damaged by what I have said, remember what I have suffered and am still suffering!"

As she said the last word she walked towards the door pulling Felicita with her.

There was a determination in the way she moved.

She held Felicita's hand so firmly that there was nothing she could do but go with her.

She was aware as she did so that the *Marques* was still sitting where they had left him.

Even if she could have looked back, she would not have seen him.

Her eyes were filled with tears.

The servants in the hall were waiting with their cloaks.

The carriage was outside and the moment they stepped into it, the horses moved off.

Now tears were running down Felicita's face and she made no attempt to prevent them.

They were both silent.

Until, as they reached the road which ran along the shore, Felicita said in a broken little voice:

"H . . . how could you . . . have told him . . .
1 . . . like that?"

"It was the truth," the *Duchesse* said, "and
now you can forget him as I intend to forget his
father!"

"I can . . . never forget . . . him!" Felicita said
brokenly.

"Nonsense!" the *Duchesse* replied sharply.
"My love lasted for five years, yours has not even
lasted for five days!"

Felicita did not answer.

She covered her face with her hands.

She was trying to prevent herself from breaking down and sobbing uncontrollably.

She had thought as the *Duchesse* spoke how
sordid and unpleasant it sounded.

The *Marques* would think that she had con-
spired with the *Duchesse* to deceive him.

He would never forgive her.

"How could I have . . . known . . . how could I
have . . . guessed," she asked herself, "that was
. . . why I had to . . . pretend to be the *Duchesse*'s
. . . niece and her . . . heiress?"

She could not prevent herself from giving a
sob which the *Duchesse* heard.

"Pull yourself together," she said sharply,
"and as you will never see the man again, the
sooner you do so, the better!"

"He will . . . not . . . want to . . . see me,"
Felicita murmured miserably.

"Of course not! He will feel humiliated that he
had not the sense to recognise you for what you

155

are! He will decide to forget the whole episode as quickly as possible."

There was a twist to the *Duchesse*'s lips as she said:

"And doubtless there will be plenty of women like the *Comtesse* to help him!"

Every word she spoke was a wound which drew blood.

Felicita did not protest, she could only cry.

They drove in silence until the *Duchesse* exclaimed:

"Here we are, and the sooner we leave Portugal and all its miseries behind, the better I shall be pleased!"

Felicita suddenly realised they had been driving for far longer than it usually took from the Palace to their house.

She took her hands from her face.

To her astonishment they were outside the Railway Station in Lisbon.

Before she could ask any questions, the carriage-door was opened.

The *Duchesse* stepped out.

A man whom Felicita had never seen before escorted them onto the platform.

There, to her astonishment, was the *Duchesse*'s lady's maid waiting at the carriage-door of a train.

It seemed different from the trains she had seen in the past.

It took her a second or two to realise they were on a side platform.

The train was so short it could only be a private one.

Pedro was also there and two other men from the Villa.

The *Duchesse* thanked Pedro and the man who had escorted them, who Felicita guessed was a Courier.

She gave him a sum of money to be distributed amongst the staff.

Then the *Duchesse* moved into the train.

Because she realised it was what was expected, Felicita followed her.

She was so bewildered that she could hardly understand what was happening.

Yet she was aware that the *Duchesse* must have had everything arranged before they had left that evening.

She supposed their luggage would have been already taken onto the train.

Now, as the *Duchesse* had said, she was leaving Portugal and the *Marques* for ever.

"I . . . cannot . . . do it! I must . . . stay . . . here . . . I must . . . stay . . . behind!" Felicita was thinking frantically.

Then she remembered that she had no money, no clothes but what she stood up in.

If the *Duchesse* had finished with the house in which they had been staying — nowhere to go.

She stood undecided in the Drawing-Room of the small train, looking helpless.

"Sit down!" the *Duchesse* commanded.

As Felicita did so the train moved off.

"Everything has been arranged as you requested, *Madame*," the Courier said in French. "Would you care for a glass of champagne, and perhaps something to eat?"

"Nothing to eat, thank you, Henri," the *Duchesse* replied, "but a glass of champagne would be pleasant, and also one for *Mademoiselle.*"

Henri left the Drawing-Room.

A few minutes later a steward wearing a white coat brought in the champagne.

He offered a glass to Felicita who took it.

She had no wish to drink, only to understand what was happening.

When the *Duchesse* had drunk a little and they were alone she said:

"I imagine you are anxious to know what is going to happen to you?"

"I . . . I am . . . frightened," Felicita admitted.

"Well, I suppose, as you played your part exactly as I wanted you to, I owe you something," the *Duchesse* said in a hard voice.

Y . . . you have been . . . very kind, *Madame,*" Felicita said hesitatingly, "b . . . but . . . I loved him!"

The *Duchesse's* lips twisted scornfully.

"As I loved his father, and a lot of good it did me!"

"I . . . I thought he . . . loved me for . . . m . . . myself."

"Then you are a fool, as I was!" the *Duchesse* retorted. "Men are all the same, and for men like

158

the *Marques* love does not count beside breeding."

Tears blinded Felicita.

In a pathetic little voice she said:

"D . . . do you mean he . . . only cared for me
because . . . he thought I was . . . your niece . . .
and you would . . . l . . . leave me money when
you . . . d . . . died?'

"He certainly would not have noticed you if he
had known who you really were!"

Felicita shut her eyes.

She felt that the *Duchesse* had struck her a mor-
tal blow.

Of course that was the truth.

How could the *Marques,* of all people, care for
a woman such as she really was?

A pedlar, like those who congregated in the
Squares, following the tourists and thrusting
their goods upon them.

Her agony was so intense that she wished she
could die.

Just as the *Duchesse* said she had died.

But the girl who had loved the *Marques*'s father had lived to become a *Duchesse* . . .

"I suppose I had better tell you," the *Duchesse*
said interrupting her thoughts, "what I have
planned. It may surprise you, but I am sending
you to England."

"To England?" Felicita exclaimed in astonishment. "B . . . but . . . I have . . . never been . . .
there!"

"I feel in a way responsible for you, although

there is no reason why I should be," the *Duchesse* said. "And there is just a chance, a very remote one, that the *Marques,* like his father, might wish to make you his mistress!"

Felicita's heart gave a leap.

If she could see him again . . . if she could explain to him what had happened . . . if he still loved her . . . even a . . . little . . .

Then she understood what the *Duchesse* was implying and she was shocked.

Of course she would never do anything so wrong or so wicked as to become any man's mistress.

Even though she loved the *Marques* with her whole heart.

Not only would her mother have been horrified, but the Virgin Mary, to whom she said her prayers, would tell her it was wrong and a sin.

Her teaching at the Convent and all her devotion to God had made her aware that to live with a man without marriage was to degrade herself.

It was also a sin beyond redemption.

In a voice that seemed to come from far away, she said

"D . . . did you . . . say, *Madame,* that you were . . . sending me to . . . England?"

"Yes, to England!" the *Duchesse* answered. "That is one place where the *Marques* will not look for you if he takes the trouble to look anywhere!"

She glanced at Felicita.

She realised how pathetic the girl looked with

tears running down her pale cheeks.

Her fingers were clasped together in an effort at self-control.

"In England I am sure you will find work of some sort to do," the *Duchesse* went on, "and certainly people will be prepared to buy what you make."

"B . . . but . . . I have . . . never been to . . . England!"

"Then it will be an experience for you," the *Duchesse* replied, "and I am being exceedingly generous. I will give you your fare money for your journey and I will also pay into a Bank in London in your name the sum of £500."

She paused but Felicita did not speak and she went on:

"With that you will not be penniless while you are trying to find something to do, or somebody to look after you."

It was generous, Felicita thought.

At the same time, she was terrified.

At least in Portugal there were people like the Lodging-house Keeper who had been kind to her.

Perhaps, although she had tried before, she would find some of her father's friends who might help her.

But England!

"Now that is settled," the *Duchesse* said, "we must go to bed and rest. We shall not arrive in Paris until late tomorrow evening, so you may as well enjoy the luxury that you do not have to pay for for as long as you can!"

She rose to her feet as she spoke.

Holding onto the back of the seat to support herself against the movement of the train, she added:

"I have the satisfaction of knowing that the *Marques* Alvaro will lie awake to-night, and I have given him a great deal to think about!"

She went from the Drawing-Room as she spoke.

She was not aware that once again Felicita had covered her face with her hands.

She was now crying despairingly.

She had awoken from her dream.

Her happiness had been shattered into a thousand pieces.

She was alone and helpless.

She had lost the most wonderful thing she had ever known — love.

The agony of her thoughts seemed to seep through her.

She slipped off the chair on which she was sitting to kneel on the floor.

She cried and cried, until it felt as if her tears overflowed through her fingers and onto the floor.

Suddenly there was a deafening explosion.

It was so startling that for a moment her tears ceased.

She was frozen into a kind of immobility.

There was another crash, and yet another.

Everything seemed to be falling around her.

As the whole floor shook she realised for one

fleeting second that the carriage was turning over.

She knew she was in a train-crash.

Then she felt the blow of something hard and heavy strike her on the head.

There was darkness and she knew no more . . .

Chapter Seven

Felicita came slowly back down a long dark tunnel.

She was lying on a cloud and she thought she must be dead.

She vaguely remembered the noise of several explosions, and a sudden violent pain in her head, then darkness.

For a long time she could not think what it could be.

Then she was vaguely aware that she had been in a train.

The *Duchesse* was taking her away from the *Marques*.

Now the agony of losing him was back in her breast, and without really intending to she opened her eyes.

She found she was in a room she had never seen before.

It was small, austere and plain.

As she stared at the white walls without any decoration, somebody rose from a chair by the window and came to the bedside.

"Are you awake?" a soft voice asked in Portuguese.

"Where . . . am . . . I?"

It was difficult to say the words.

Felicita was not certain whether she spoke them aloud or merely that her lips moved.

"You are quite safe, and you are in hospital," the voice replied.

Then a gentle hand lifted her head and a cup was held to her lips.

She swallowed what it contained and the quiet voice said:

"Go to sleep. You are quite safe, and you will feel better when you wake."

Because it was easier to obey than to think, Felicita did as she was told.

When Felicita awoke again it was night and a Nun was tidying her bed.

She did not speak for some minutes, then the Nun said:

"Is there anything you want? Are you thirsty?"

"I . . . I . . . think I . . . am."

The Nun brought her something to drink.

It made Felicita feel a little stronger, so that she asked:

"Am I . . . injured from what I . . . think must have been a . . . train-crash?"

The Nun, who was quite elderly gave her a smile.

"You were very fortunate, my child. The Good Lord looked after you and you are uninjured."

"My . . . my . . . head," Felicita managed to say.

"You suffered a little concussion, but the skin was not broken and you will soon feel yourself again. But now you must go to sleep."

Felicita shut her eyes, but she did not sleep for a little while.

She was saying a prayer to the Blessed Virgin to thank Her, as she knew she ought to do.

At the same time, she was praying that the *Marques* would not forget her.

It was morning when Felicita next awoke.

She was washed, her hair brushed, and she was propped up against a number of pillows.

A little later the Doctor arrived.

He was a middle-aged man with a kind face and he said when he looked down at her:

"You are a very fortunate young woman!"

"I . . . I am grateful . . . that I am not . . . injured," Felicita replied.

"Or dead!" he added.

"Were . . . people . . . killed in the . . . crash?"

As she asked the question she realised that neither the Doctor nor the Nun who was with him wished to reply.

Instead he said hastily:

"Sister Benedict tells me that you have had a good night and been a very good patient. I will come and see you to-morrow."

He turned to the Nun.

"She is to be kept quiet, no visitors, no talking, and try to persuade her to eat."

Then he was gone before Felicita had a chance

166

to ask him anything else.

At the same time she felt apprehensive.

Supposing something had happened to the *Duchesse?*

If she was very ill, or perhaps dead, what was she to do?

It was wrong to think of herself, but she remembered the *Duchesse* had said she was sending her to England.

Once again she was frightened.

She wanted to have the opportunity of pleading with the *Duchesse* to let her stay in Portugal.

If she was ill it might prove impossible to do so.

Sister Benedict came back into the room and Felicita said:

"Please . . . Sister, I want to know . . . exactly what has . . . happened."

"You heard what the Doctor said," the Nun replied, "and you know I have to obey his orders."

She saw the disappointment in Felicita's eyes and added kindly:

"Be grateful that God has protected you and your face is not scarred."

As if she felt Felicita was still worrying, she added:

"One of the Nuns said that when you were asleep you looked like an angel!"

Then she lowered the blind to keep out the sunshine and went from the room.

Felicita tried to pray.

All she could think of was that she was alone and afraid.

Without really meaning to she found herself begging the *Marques* to help her.

"You loved me . . . I know you loved . . . me a . . . little," she said as if to convince herself, "and now I . . . need you to look . . . after me . . . to help me . . . and tell . . . me what . . . to do."

She gave a little sob before she continued:

"I will . . . not be a . . . nuisance . . . I will not . . . impose upon you . . . but there is . . . no one else who will . . . understand how . . . helpless I . . . feel."

It suddenly struck her that if she was in a hospital in a room to herself, she would have to pay.

How could she make the Nuns understand that she had no money?

Although she was sure they would be kind and charitable, they would think it very strange.

They would know that she had been travelling in a private train and was richly dressed.

"I must . . . find out . . . about the *Duchesse*," she thought, "and when she is . . . well enough . . . I must see . . . her and . . . talk to her."

She had heard the hard note in the *Duchesse*'s voice when she told her she had to go to England.

She knew it would be very embarrassing to make other demands when she had been so generous.

She told herself she should be very grateful for the food she had eaten with the *Duchesse*.

For the clothes she had given her.

Even though she had been deceitful, she had met the *Marques*.

At the thought of him tears came into her eyes.

But instead of crying, she pretended that he had his arms around her so that she was no longer afraid.

"I . . . love you . . . I love . . . you!" she whispered and fell asleep.

Felicita must have slept for several hours.

Then when she was still dreaming, the door opened. She heard Sister Benedict say in a whisper:

"She is asleep, and you must not waken her."

"No, of course not," a man's voice answered.

Realising who it was, Felicita opened her eyes.

It was the *Marques* who stood there, looking just as she had been dreaming of him.

She gave a cry of joy.

He moved swiftly across the room and she held out her arms.

"You are awake!" he exclaimed. "Are you in any pain?"

There was so much anxiety in his voice that she felt her heart turn over in her breast.

Not only because he was there, but because he cared.

"I . . . I am all . . . right, and . . . I was dreaming."

Sister Benedict shut the door.

The *Marques* sat down on the side of the bed as

169

he had sat on the couch in the Saloon of the yacht.

"They would not let me see you yesterday or the day before," he said, "but I pleaded with the Doctor, and he allowed me to come in this afternoon."

"Y . . . you have . . . been here . . . all that time?" Felicita murmured.

She was trying to understand what was happening.

"When I heard of the crash," the *Marques* said, "I thought I would go mad! The only information in the newspapers was that several people had been killed or mortally injured."

"The . . . *Duchesse?*" Felicita questioned.

The *Marques* hesitated but the pressure of his hands on hers increased as he said very quietly:

"The *Duchesse* was killed."

"How . . . terrible!"

"It was only by a miracle that you were saved!"

"A . . . miracle?"

"In some strange way one of the arm-chairs in the carriage fell over the top of you. They did not find you for a long time, but the chair protected you when the train fell down the bank. The roof caved in killing almost everybody except yourself."

Felicita clung to him as if he was a lifeline to prevent her from drowning.

"So . . . I was . . . saved!"

"For which I have thanked God a million times since I arrived here."

"Y . . . you . . . you came . . . to see . . . me?"

"I came to tell you that I love you."

She stared at him as if she had not heard him aright.

Then it was as if a thousand candles had been lit inside her eyes.

"Y . . . you . . . love me?"

"You know I love you! How dare you doubt my love and go away in that cruel, heartless fashion?"

"I . . . did not know what was . . . happening . . . I had no idea . . . there was a . . . train waiting to take . . . us to . . . Paris."

"We need not talk about that now," the *Marques* said. "All I want to do is to tell you that I love you and make sure you love me."

"I . . . love you . . . I do . . . love you!" Felicita replied. "But . . . I thought you would be . . . angry because I had . . . deceived you."

"All I can think of at the moment is that you are alive," the *Marques* said. "When I thought you were dead, I knew I had lost the only thing that matters to me in the whole world!"

"It . . . cannot be . . . true what you are . . . saying!" Felicita whispered.

Her voice broke as tears filled her eyes.

The *Marques* lifted her head and kissed it.

"This is too much for you," he said, "we will talk about it another time when you are stronger."

She thought he was about to leave her and hung onto him.

171

"Stay . . . with me . . . please . . . stay with me," she begged. "I have been . . . praying that . . . you would understand . . . and know how . . . frightened I am."

"There is nothing to frighten you," the *Marques* said, "and you must get well quickly, so that we can be married."

Felicita was very still.

Her eyes sought his as if she was not certain that she had heard what he said.

"M . . . married?" she stammered.

"That is what we were planning to do when you ran away."

"B . . . but . . . but the *Duchesse* . . . told you . . . what I . . . was."

The *Marques* smiled.

"To me you are everything I have longed for, looked for, and was quite convinced did not exist."

"But . . . she said . . . you could . . . never marry me . . . as your father would not marry her."

"I am not concerned with my father or the *Duchesse*," the *Marques* said. "You are mine, and we are going to be married as soon as you are well enough to leave here and come back to the Palace."

"I . . . I do not . . . believe it!"

Now the tears ran down her cheeks.

"If you cry, my precious," the *Marques* said, "they will send me away and be very angry with me."

The way he spoke made her give a little choked laugh.

He took his fine lawn handkerchief from his pocket and wiped her eyes.

He kissed her cheeks, first one then the other, very, very gently.

It was as if he was touching a flower, then he kissed her lips.

To Felicita, it was as if the Heavens themselves opened.

She was swept from a despond of misery and fear into a blinding light, which came from the *Marques*.

She knew it was the light of love.

"I . . . love you . . . I love . . . you!" she whispered.

Then as he was looking down at her as if he had never seen her before she managed to say:

"B . . . but you . . . must not . . . marry me!"

"Why not?"

"Because . . . you might be . . . ashamed of me and I . . . would lose you . . . then I would . . . want to die . . . as the *Duchesse* . . . tried to do."

"You are not to talk like that," the *Marques* said firmly. "I have found out about this extraordinary story, and I cannot believe it is not something straight out of a novel."

"You . . . know about . . . it?"

"A great deal more than the *Duchesse* told us the other night."

"Then, tell me . . . please . . . tell me!" Felicita begged.

"You do not know what happened?"

173

"I knew . . . nothing."

She paused.

She could not look at the *Marques* as she went on in a voice he could hardly hear:

"It was . . . true that I . . . met her in the . . . Grand Hotel . . . when I was trying to sell the . . . needlework I had learnt to do at the Convent . . . where I was educated."

He did not speak and after a moment she went on:

"As she said . . . I was a . . . pedlar."

"That is something you will never be again," the *Marques* answered.

He bent forward to kiss her forehead.

"It sounds so . . . horrible and . . . humiliating," Felicita faltered, "but . . . I had no money . . . after Mama . . . died, and I thought I would . . . die of . . . starvation."

"I saw how thin you were when I first met you," the *Marques* remarked, "but how could I have guessed when you were introduced as the niece of the *Duchesse,* who is a very rich woman, that you had been without food?"

"The *Duchesse* . . . was very . . . kind to . . . me," Felicita replied, "and when she said she wanted me to . . . pretend to be her niece . . . I had no idea why."

She looked up at the *Marques* piteously as she went on:

"You do . . . believe me? When the *Duchesse* told you who I . . . really was after you had told her you . . . loved me, that was the . . . first time I

174

had any . . . idea that the . . . pretence was intended to . . . hurt you because . . . she had been . . . hurt by your . . . father."

"Of course I believe you," the *Marques* said, "but, my precious, you will never lie to me again, just as you will never leave me!"

"And you . . . really mean to . . . marry me?"

"The very moment that you are well enough to leave here."

Felicita gave a little murmur of excitement. Then she said:

"You will think it very . . . stupid of me, but I have no . . . idea where I am, except that . . . since the Nuns are Portuguese I presume I am still . . . in Portugal."

"You are in the Convent of the Sacred Heart at Oporto," the *Marques* said, "and the Hospital is attached to the Convent."

Felicita gave a little sigh of contentment as she said:

"I am so . . . glad I am . . . still in my own . . . country . . . and now that I am with you . . . I do not . . . have to go to . . . England."

"To England?" the Marques exclaimed in surprise.

"That was . . . where the *Duchesse* was sending me, so that even if you ever . . . wanted to find me . . . you would not be . . . able to."

He put his arms round her as he said:

"I would have found you wherever you had hidden yourself! I will never lose you, my beautiful darling, and I swear that you will never lose me!"

Because he could not help himself, he kissed her.

His lips were gentle and very tender.

Only when he felt Felicita quiver against him did he say:

"Now I am really going to leave you, and as soon as you are well enough I will take you home."

"H . . . home?" Felicita questioned.

"To our home, yours and mine, my darling."

He kissed her again.

It was difficult for Felicita to sleep that night because she was so excited.

Yet she found it hard to believe she was not dreaming.

Could it really be true that he intended her to be his wife after all the *Duchesse* had said?

It was only after he left her that she had realised she had not told him anything about herself.

Unless he was clairvoyant, he knew nothing about her.

Except that she had been, according to the *Duchesse*, a Portuguese pedlar.

Yet he said he intended to make her his wife.

"Could any . . . man be more . . . wonderful?" she asked aloud.

Then she was praying, prayers of gratitude that came from the very depths of her soul.

The Virgin Mary had blessed her and proved that love was greater than anything that was material.

Greater even than the pride of the *Marques* Alvaro.

Felicita was dressed in her own clothes which had been brought to the Convent from the wrecked train.

Her trunks had fortunately been undamaged.

She still knew very little about the crash for the Nuns would not speak of it.

Sister Benedict told her that the *Marques* had said he would be responsible for her learning all that was necessary.

"He will look after you," Sister Benedict added, "and I pray that you will never again be in such a dreadful and terrifying accident."

She had helped Felicita into a pretty gown the colour of her eyes.

With it she wore a small hat trimmed with flowers and velvet ribbons.

Then Felicita had sat waiting for the *Marques*.

He came in, and she rose slowly to her feet.

They were alone and he took her into his arms.

He held her very close before he said:

"You are all right? This is not too much for you?"

"I only want to . . . be with . . . you."

She knew by the expression in his eyes that was what he wanted to hear.

He kissed her again.

Then as he turned towards the door she said:

"Please . . . I have . . . something to ask you."

He waited and she said:

"The *Duchesse* said she was . . . arranging to give me some . . . money in England . . . and also paying my fare . . . but I have no . . . money of my own. But . . . I would like to . . . give some to the . . . Convent . . . to thank them . . ."

She felt embarrassed at having to ask him for money.

Yet she could think of no other way to express her gratitude for the way in which the Nuns had looked after her.

The *Marques* smiled.

"I have already done that," he said, "and I assure you, the Nuns were very grateful."

Felicita made a little murmur and pressed her cheek against his shoulder.

"I might have . . . guessed that . . . you would think of . . . everything."

"I thought of you, and that you are alive," the *Marques* answered. "Come, my darling, let us go home!"

They travelled back in a carriage that had been attached to a fast train that ran between Oporto and Lisbon.

The *Marques* very quietly told Felicita about the crash.

The *Duchesse* had insisted that her private train should leave immediately she boarded it.

The line however had not been as clear as it should have been.

Ten miles outside Oporto the small train had crashed head on into a Goods Train coming in the opposite direction.

The drivers of both trains were killed.

When the private train overturned, the roof had caved in, killing the *Duchesse,* Henri and a steward.

Four other men, including the Guard on the train were badly injured.

One of them lost a leg.

As Felicita listened to what the *Marques* was telling her she realised it was her tears that had saved her.

Because she had been crying so tempestuously, she had crouched down on the floor.

The arm-chair had toppled over to shield her.

It had rendered her unconscious.

But it had protected her from the flying glass and the shattered roof.

Other wreckage had crashed down and killed five people on the train.

The *Marques* told her he had offered to help the men who had been injured but were still alive.

He had made all the arrangements for the *Duchesse*'s body to be taken to France.

The Funeral would take place in the Chapel attached to the *Duc*'s Chateau on the Loire.

"There she will lie with all the other *Duchesses* de Monreuil," the *Marques* said, "and I feel it would give her satisfaction to know that she is far more important than if she had been my father's wife."

He was speaking lightly to prevent Felicita from being too unhappy over what had occurred.

But she said in a serious little voice:

"She must have . . . loved your father very . . . deeply."

"I am sure she did."

Then as if he thought it would divert Felicita's mind, he said:

"When you left me after the *Duchesse* had revealed how she had planned to revenge herself on my father through me, I admit I was at first stunned."

Felicita raised her eyes to his as he went on:

"I found it hard to believe the truth of what she was saying."

"But . . . you *did* . . . believe . . . it?"

"To make sure it was not some strange quirk of her imagination I went to my father's private desk, which I had never before investigated," the *Marques* replied. "It had been kept locked after his death but now I opened the drawers."

Felicita moved so that her head was on his shoulder.

He knew she was listening intently as he continued:

"I found his diary which told me what a very big part the *Duchesse* had played in his life for five years."

He paused before he said:

"I also found the cuttings from the newspapers reporting her death."

"So she . . . did deceive . . . everybody into . . . thinking she had . . . killed herself!"

"They found her clothes and her jewellery on the cliffs in a place where, if anyone fell into the sea, it would be impossible for them to survive."

"Was your father upset?" Felicita asked.

"I think," the *Marques* replied, "he was conscience-stricken for the rest of his life."

As if Felicita asked the next question without putting it into words, he said:

"At the same time, he was very happy with my mother. As you know, she was English, and very beautiful. She fell very much in love with him."

He was silent before he added:

"When I look back to when I was a small boy, the Palace days seemed to be filled with love and that, my darling, is what I want for our children."

He saw the colour come into Felicita's face.

Her eyes were very shy and he thought it was impossible for any woman to look so lovely.

It was as if it re-assured him that she was as pure and innocent as she looked.

He told himself that whatever the *Duchesse* might have said, Felicita's beauty and her intrinsic goodness made her his equal.

When they reached the Palace the *Marques* insisted Felicita should go to bed.

"I . . . I do not want to . . . leave you," she murmured.

"To stay in the Palace with me would be unconventional," he replied. "So my grandmother

181

is here to chaperon you until we are married. But I hope you will allow me to come and say good-night to you."

"Your grandmother!" Felicita exclaimed with surprise.

"She is English, and she has not been at all well, so she has been staying in a Villa by the sea."

He saw by Felicita's expression that she was nervous, and added:

"She is a very kind person, and I know she will welcome you as my future wife."

"She will . . . think I am not . . . good enough for . . . you!" Felicita said in a low voice.

"When she meets you," he replied, "I am quite certain she will think that I am not good enough for you!"

Felicita laughed because it was so absurd, and he said:

"Come and meet her, then you must go to bed."

The Duchess was, as the *Marques* had said, very old, but she still had traces of the beauty that had been hers when she was young.

She also had a presence which Felicita was sure was due to her Royal blood.

Her eyes were kind, and so was the smile she gave Felicita as she curtsied to her.

"My grandson tells me you are to be married," she said in English, "and I am overjoyed that he has at last chosen a wife."

"I . . . only hope . . . Ma'am," Felicita said,

"that I can make him . . . happy."

She spoke without even thinking about it in English.

The Duchess gave an exclamation of surprise.

"You speak English very well!"

"Thank you, Ma'am, but I have . . . never been to . . . England."

"Then my grandson must certainly bring you to stay with his English relatives who are all very fond of him."

The *Marques* would not allow them to talk for long but took Felicita upstairs.

He handed her over to the Housekeeper, who had been at the Palace for many years.

With the help of one of the maids, who she was told would look after her in future, Felicita undressed.

Then she got into bed in the most magnificent and beautiful room she had ever seen.

It looked over the countryside.

She thought how she and the *Marques* had stood under the stars and she had known how greatly she loved him.

The room, with its exquisitely carved and gilt furniture, had been used by all the Châtelaines of the Palace.

The bed had a canopy of golden cupids holding up the curtains of pale blue velvet.

She was sure that everything around her was an illusion.

She would wake up in the sordid attic of the lodginghouse where she had slept until the

Duchesse had rescued her.

Now she was alive and the *Marques* loved her, it all seemed impossible.

Later, after she had been brought a delicious dinner on a tray, the *Marques* came to say good-night to her.

Because he was determined to obey the conventions Felicita saw that he left the door open.

He walked across the room to the bedside.

"You are comfortable, my darling?" he asked.

Her eyes were shining and seemed to fill her whole face.

She held out her arms to him.

"I keep wondering if I am awake . . . or dreaming," she said. "I want to . . . touch you . . . to know that you are . . . real."

The *Marques* laughed and sat down on the bed.

"I will prove that I am real after we are married tomorrow."

"To-morrow?"

"I cannot wait any longer, and my grandmother wishes to return to the Villa. She is afraid that as the Palace is so high it may affect her asthma."

"And . . . I can really . . . marry you . . . to-morrow?"

"You will be my wife," the *Marques* said, "and after that there will be no tears and I know we will be very very happy."

He was looking into her eyes as he spoke.

She thought she saw a little flicker of fire in his.

Something within her leapt towards him.

She wanted him to kiss her as he had before, fiercely and demandingly, as if he wanted to conquer her.

Yet she realised he was holding himself strictly under control.

After a moment he said:

"There is one thing I have not yet done, my precious, and it seems extraordinary, but no more extraordinary than anything else about you."

"What is . . . it?" Felicita asked.

"Do you realise," he said, "that I actually do not know your name?"

Because it sounded so ridiculous Felicita laughed.

"No one would believe you if you told them!"

"I must have your name for the Marriage Certificate and for the family tree."

Felicita drew in her breath.

"My father was . . . Louis Manuel Galvão."

"The poet?" the *Marques* questioned.

Felicita gave a little cry.

"You have . . . heard of . . . him?"

"You will find his books in the Library."

She clasped her hands together.

"Oh, how wonderful! I know Papa would be very proud!

"I was brought up by my Tutors to read the poets of Portugal."

"As I was!" Felicita exclaimed.

"That is another thing we have in common,"

the *Marques* smiled, "and I understand now, because your father wrote so well, and his poems express beauty, why his daughter is so beautiful."

"That is a lovely thing to say!"

"And who was your mother?"

Felicita hesitated and now the *Marques* realised that something was wrong.

He waited, his eyes on her face and after a moment she said:

"I . . . I am afraid . . . when I tell you . . . you will be . . . shocked . . . as I am sure your . . . grandmother will be."

"Shocked?" the *Marques* questioned.

Then he said:

"We love each other, Felicita, and nothing and nobody shall spoil our love."

"Mama said I was . . . never to speak of it . . . because she had . . . caused such a . . . scandal."

The *Marques* did not reply, he only reached out and took Felicita's hands in his.

"M . . . my grandfather," Felicita began in a low voice, "lived near Stratford-Upon-Avon."

"The town connected with Shakespeare?" the *Marques* asked.

Felicita nodded.

"It was arranged nineteen years ago in 1871 that a party of poets and authors should visit Stratford-Upon-Avon for the celebrations which were to take place on William Shakespeare's birthday . . ."

"That is something which I believe has happened ever since," the *Marques* interrupted, "but, go on."

"My father was very proud to be one of the poets chosen to represent Portugal. When he arrived in England, because they were quite a large party, he found they were accommodated in various different houses in the neighbourhood."

Felicita paused for a moment before she continued:

"My father was sent with three other Portuguese to stay with the Earl of Stratford."

The *Marques* stiffened, then after a moment's silence he asked:

"Are you telling me that your grandfather was the Earl of Stratford?"

"Yes," Felicita answered, "but . . . I have not . . . finished the . . . story."

She did not look at the *Marques* as she continued in a very low voice:

"Mama was engaged to the eldest son of the Duke of Ilminster, and they were to be married in a week's time."

The *Marques* already guessed what had happened.

But he did not interrupt again as Felicita went on:

"She said that the moment she saw Papa she knew he was the man who had always been in her . . . dreams."

"And so they fell in love," the *Marques* said quietly.

"They knew they could not . . . live without . . .

each other, so . . . they ran away."

She looked up at the *Marques* as she spoke, beseeching him to understand.

He was smiling as he bent forward, his lips very near to hers as he said:

"So, very sensibly, they ran away, my darling, just as I would have asked you to run away with me, if there had been another man in your life!"

"You . . . understand?" Felicita asked, "you . . . really understand?"

"Of course I understand, and I thought I had already proved to you that love is more important than anything else."

"And . . . you still wanted to . . . m . . . marry me when you did not even . . . know my name! How could . . . anyone be so magnificent . . . so utterly and completely . . . wonderful?"

Her voice broke.

The *Marques* was kissing her fiercely and demandingly, as she wanted him to do.

Only when they were both breathless did he say:

"My precious, why are you so poor? Could you not have gone to England? I cannot believe your relatives would not have looked after you."

"I once suggested it to Mama after Papa died . . . but she said her father would . . . never forgive her for having caused such a scandal."

Felicita lowered her voice.

"The Queen was to have been represented at her wedding, the presents had all arrived, and there were two younger members of the Royal

Family among her bride's maids."

The *Marques* laughed and it was a very happy sound.

"I can see, my darling, that your mother flouted all the conventions of British protocol, and I admire her for her bravery more than I can ever say."

"I wish Mama . . . could have . . . known . . . that!"

"I am sure she does," the *Marques* said quietly.

He saw the happiness in Felicita's eyes.

He knew it was because she loved him and was so grateful to him for understanding.

Her mother had felt that the advantages of being a Duchess were of no consequence beside the emotions of the heart.

That was what he understood.

It was what he felt himself, and he had been prepared to marry Felicita whatever she was.

Even, as the *Duchesse* had said, nothing but a Portuguese pedlar.

He knew now that with his grandmother's help, Felicita's Stratford relations would undoubtedly welcome her into the family.

What was more, Felicita would grace her traditional place at the Court of King Carlos.

Because she was so unspoilt and so unsophisticated, she did not understand.

He had, however, no intention of letting her realise the difference this would mean to her in the future.

He had been prepared to protect her from any

of the problems which might arise because she was his wife.

At the same time, it would have been impossible to avoid them completely.

Or for her to be immune from the spitefulness of envious tongues and the chatter of jealous women.

Like Felicita, the *Marques* said a prayer of gratitude.

He had mocked at his father for being so insistent that the woman he married must be worthy of his name, and her blood as good as his own.

Nevertheless, he could understand his pride.

It had made the *Marques* Juan marry an English noblewoman while he still loved Inès.

Felicita was saying:

"Mama had a very small income from her grandmother which kept us from starving while she was alive."

She gave a deep sigh.

"But that ceased when she . . . died."

The *Marques* bent forward to kiss her again, saying as he did so:

"All you have to think about to-night, and this is an order, is that you love me, and to-morrow we will be married."

His voice deepened as he said slowly:

"We will begin a life of such happiness in our enchanted Palace that our love will reach out to help other people to be as happy as we are."

"That is . . . what I want to do," Felicita said. "Promise me you will not . . . vanish in the night and . . . leave me alone."

"I promise I shall be here in the morning," the *Marques* smiled, "and after that we will be together by day and by night!"

He kissed her very gently, then rising to his feet he kissed both her hands.

"Good-night, my beautiful wife-to-be," he said, "and God bless you, as already He has blessed us both."

Felicita gave him a shy little smile.

Then as he went from the room and shut the door behind him, she clasped her hands together and shut her eyes.

"Thank You . . . God . . . thank You!" she said over and over again.

Then she added a little secret prayer.

"Please, Mary, Mother of God, give us sons who will be as fine and as handsome, kind and gentle as he is so that the people who look up to the Palace will be inspired by those who own it as they were by Your Holy and Blessed Son."

Felicita was married at noon the following day.

The little Chapel was attached to the East Wing of the Palace.

The only witnesses were the Duchess and the *Marques*'s secretary who had been with him for many years.

There were two young servers to assist the elderly Chaplain.

The fragrance of incense mingled with the

scent of the arum lilies which filled the Chapel.

Felicita wore the same white and silver gown she had worn the first evening she had come to the Palace.

The evening when the *Marques* had fallen in love with her and she with him.

Over her head, but not over her face, she wore an ancient lace veil that had been in the family for many years.

Her wreath was of real orange-blossom, made for her by the gardeners.

She carried just a few perfect Madonna lilies in her arms.

When she came into the Chapel the *Marques* was waiting for her.

He thought she might have stepped out of one of the stained-glass windows and was a Saint or an angel.

Yet as she slipped her hand into his he knew she was human.

He loved her with all his heart and, although it was something he had never expected, also with his soul.

After the Marriage Service was over and they had received the Communion, they knelt for the Blessing.

Then both Felicita and the *Marques* felt there was a sudden light in the Chapel.

It was not sunshine, but something very much more brilliant.

So vivid that they were almost blinded by it.

It was the Blessing of God.

They walked out into the garden, the sun was shining on the fountains, Felicita knew that their love had transformed the Palace into a very special Paradise.

As the *Marques* had said, it would bring happiness to a great number of people besides themselves.

After luncheon a carriage carried the *Marques*'s grandmother away to her Villa near the sea.

They were alone and the *Marques* took Felicita out onto the terrace.

"In a few minutes," he said, "we are going upstairs for our *siesta*. But first, I wanted you, my darling, to look down from our Palace in the Clouds and tell me that you are happy to be here, and are no longer afraid."

"I shall . . . never be . . . afraid as long as . . . you are . . . with me."

Far away in the distance she could see Lisbon.

She felt, although it was impossible, that she could see too the little house where she had lived with her parents.

She moved a little nearer to the *Marques* as she said:

"Sometimes I wish that . . . you were not so . . . important or so rich . . . so that I could . . . show you that I love you . . . just as a man."

She put her head against his shoulder.

"If we had to live . . . as you say . . . down below . . . I would look after you . . . and of course

193

. . . love you . . . just as much . . . if not more than
I do now."

She knew the *Marques* was moved by what she
had said.

As his arms tightened he said:

"Do you suppose, my precious, that I do not
know that? But I still like to hear you say it. Our
love is greater than poverty, greater than privation, greater than anything else in the world!"

He touched her hair with his lips before he
went on:

"The first time I brought you here you said it
made you feel as if you were God, looking down
on the world you had created."

His voice deepened:

"That is what I feel. I have battled against
strange and unexpected difficulties to find you,
and at last you are mine!"

There was a fire in his eyes as he added:

"What are we waiting for? I want, my precious,
adorable, little wife, to teach you about love, and
there is a great deal for you to learn."

Felicita drew in her breath.

"As you say . . . my wonderful, magnificent
husband . . . what are we . . . waiting for?"

The *Marques* gave a little laugh.

Taking Felicita by the hand he drew her back
through the Salon and up the stairs.

When they reached her bed-room the sunshine was streaming through the windows in a
golden light.

Because it was so lovely she felt as if it filled

her heart and flickered through her body.

Then as she turned towards the *Marques* she was in his arms.

He was kissing her fiercely, wildly, passionately.

She could feel the sun burning on his lips, as it was burning in her breast.

"I . . . love you . . . I love you!"

She said the words in her mind, in her heart, and in her soul.

Then there was only the sunshine which had turned to flames, the *Marques*'s arms, his lips — and him.

The employees of G.K. Hall hope you have enjoyed this Large Print book. All our Large Print titles are designed for easy reading, and all our books are made to last. Other G.K. Hall books are available at your library, through selected book-stores, or directly from us.

For information about titles, please call:

(800) 257-5157

To share your comments, please write:

Publisher
G.K. Hall & Co.
P.O. Box 159
Thorndike, ME 04986